NO QUARTER

They finally broke Miguel after four hours in the blazing sun. They had stripped him naked, then staked him out on the ground. Each wrist and ankle had been bound to pegs with leather thongs which slowly contracted under the sun's searing heat in a violent ecstasy of pain.

In the end the Mexican went mad and they plucked the information they wanted from him.

The tough Texans hunting El Lupo, the sadistic guerrilla chieftain who was trying to grab the Spread Eagle Ranch, knew what to expect. They would suffer even more than Miguel if they fell into El Lupo's hands.

This was total war with no quarter given on either side. And a man was better off as a corpse than as a prisoner.

AUTHOR'S PROFILE

Ken Hamlin is the pseudonym of a well known writer of hard cover and paperback books. A graduate of Dartmouth, he saw extensive service with the Marines during World War II.

After the war he worked as an investigator for a detective agency, then spent three years as a copywriter with an advertising agency before joining the advertising department of Warner Brothers. Subsequently he left Warners to become a full-time writer.

A Western Novel

GUNS OF REVENGE

Ken Hamlin

WILDSIDE PRESS

To
C. C. Wintermute, of the West

Cover Painting by A. Leslie Ross

ONE

Bogan was in deep sleep one moment and awake the next
—awake and gazing somberly into the barrel of a gun.
He thought, *A man caught in his own damn blankets
deserves no better.* . . .

"You got food?" he was asked by a voice so tense and
desperate it nearly cracked. Bogan shook his head
slightly.

"Not much," he admitted.

"Enough for the two of us?"

Bogan, after his fashion, considered that before answer-
ing. "No," he said.

The gunhammer clicked open.

"Your tough luck, friend," the voice told him and
Bogan sighed deeply, regretfully, watched the gunbarrel
dip slightly and level off at his mouthline. He decided,
knowing it was a small vanity, to die with his eyes closed
—and hard on that decision came the explosion that tore
the night's black silence wide open. A scream of pain and
shocked surprise was its echo.

Bogan rolled with animal instinct at the first sound,
came to a kneeling position with the second to find his
would-be assassin writhing wounded in the grass and
groaning with agony.

From the deepest shadows of the camp site stepped
Conerley, the smoke still curling from the ancient scatter-
gun he carried before him.

"That was pretty close," he commented, reloading as he
advanced.

"That was pretty *damn* close," Bogan told him in repri-
mand. "How'd he get by you?"

Conerley grinned, sheepishly, tugged at his ear lobe
with a free hand.

"Dozed off, I guess," he confessed. "So sleepy quiet
around here." He spoke conversationally, and as he spoke

5

he was raising the big greener to his shoulder, sighting down at the moaning intruder.

"Now what are you going to do?" Bogan asked and his partner glanced over at him in surprise.

"Gonna finish him off," Conerley said. "Put him out of his friggin' misery."

"Let's have a look at him first."

"Look at him later."

Bogan had risen from his knees, risen to a prodigious height, and now walked squarely into Conerley's line of fire. He knelt again.

"Can you hear me, mister?" he asked.

The answer was an unintelligible whimper.

"You bad hit?" Bogan asked. "In the vitals?"

The man only groaned, and at Bogan's back came an exasperated sigh.

"Oh, for crissake, Jess—get out of the way!" Conerley demanded. "It wasn't a minute ago that jasper was primed to open a hole in your head!"

Bogan ignored him, laid his shaggy head against the wounded man's thin chest and listened gravely for a heartbeat.

"Light a fire, Beau," he said.

"A *fire?* Man, are you loco?"

"Light a fire," Bogan said again.

"What in hell for? I thought we was avoidin' *Federales,* not advertisin' for 'em. . . ."

Bogan stood up, his wide-shouldered tallness seeming to challenge the very trees, and strode toward the small pile of wood that was to cook their meager meal in the morning.

"All right, all right," Beau Conerley complained, lowering the greener. "The damnedest, softest-headed hombre I ever run with—that's you!" His voice went on, querulously, but he got the fire blazing and by its light Bogan saw that their luckless visitor had caught a sizable load of buckshot along his left side.

"Messy gun to use on a man," he commented, ripping away the man's already tattered shirtsleeve and baring the bloody arm.

"You'd druther I'd of held my fire?" Conerley in-

6

quired and Jess Bogan raised his quiet gaze, grinned broadly at his best friend. It was as though a warm light had been turned on, and Conerley's impatient belligerence melted away.

"Come kneel on his shoulders, Beau," Jess Bogan said. "Hold him still while I dig the lead out." Conerley moved to obey and then the man on the ground spoke up.

"Don't let me die," he pleaded. "Please—don't let me die. . . ."

Conerley set himself astride the man's shoulders, and a moment later had to bear down with all his might to keep the screaming victim prone while Bogan's blade pried loose the buckshot imbedded in his flesh.

"Damn sidewinder—stop your squallin'!" Conerley shouted down at him. Bogan worked on, imperturbably, surely, and when the noise and suffering all around him seemed to be rising to an intolerable crescendo his patient mercifully passed out.

"What the hell—did he die?" Beau asked indignantly.

"Not yet," Jess said.

"Sure beats me—takin' all this trouble, riskin' a fire—all for a snake that was writin' your ticket."

"Maybe you and me never got that hungry, Beau."

"No? How hungry *can* you get? I'd never kill a man just to feed my belly."

"You're the gentle kind," Bogan told him good-humoredly, retieing the loose shirtsleeve around the arm in lieu of a better bandage. He got to his feet then, stared down at the unconscious man thoughtfully as he fished his pocket for tobacco and papers. "Looks licked, don't he?" he said. "Looks like a poor son that's come to the end of the string."

Conerley studied the man he had shot, saw someone of forty-odd—old by his standards—medium-tall, emaciated of face and body, a growth of straw-blond hair that straggled to his neckline, a wispy beard and limp mustache.

"Looks like another bum to me," Conerley said and Bogan laughed.

"Wait till he gets his first good look at us," he said. "We sure don't look like that."

Bogan glanced down at the smaller man, laughed anew.

7

"We don't win the blue ribbon, I tell you that." He threw an enormous arm around Conerley's shoulder. "Go turn in," he told him and began kicking dirt over the fire, killing it.

"Turn in, hell," Conerley shot back. "You got three, four hours coming." He spat at a tongue of flame still flickering. "I won't let you down a second time."

"Ain't been a first time, Beau."

"But, Jesus, that was close. I can still hear him thumbing that hammer. . . ."

"Hit your blankets," Bogan said. "I'm wide awake."

"You sure?"

"I'm sure."

Beau turned in, fell asleep almost immediately. Bogan took his own blankets and covered the wounded man, picked up the handgun from where it had fallen and looked it over curiously. This was a make he had never seen before, a foreign gun, and damn well put together. He wondered then if the man himself wasn't foreign—and wondered what you had to go through to hold another man's life so cheap. He stuck the gun inside his own waistband, reflecting that the visitor would be even hungrier come morning.

Bogan snubbed out the cigarette with his boot heel and moved off into the shadows, sat down with his broad back propped against a tree and resumed the watch for the rest of the night. For they were still in Mexico, aliens in a hostile, *yanqui*-hating land, and California was another long day's journey north.

2

"Come and get it, Jess," Beau Conerley called and Bogan pushed himself stiffly to his feet, walked back into the clearing where Conerley was cooking. The sun was a red ball on the eastern horizon of a cloudless sky and already the chill and dampness of the night were burning off.

"Another scorcher," Conerley said.

Bogan yawned mightily, then suddenly swung around, as if remembering something. The visitor had moved from the place where he had been lying last night. Now he was on the furthest fringe, sitting crosslegged, hollow-eyed, looking for all the world like his own skeleton.

"Mornin'," Bogan greeted him but there was no acknowledgment. The man only stared fixedly at the butt of the gun protruding from the tall man's waist.

"How's the arm?" Bogan asked and again there was no answer.

"He's been sittin' there like that since I woke up," Conerley said. "Gives me the friggin' creeps."

"What's on the menu?"

"The other jackrabbit from yesterday. Been boilin' the sonofabitch for an hour and he still don't cut."

"The rattler's all gone?"

"Gone is right. Gone maggoty. I swear, Jess, these critters in Mexico are bound and determined to get you whether they're dead or alive."

"Hack me a hind leg of that bunny," Bogan said, then carried the lean, sinewy meat to the seated man. "It's not much," he told him. "Like I mentioned last night."

The stranger gazed at the offering balefully for a long moment, then reached out with his good hand and snatched the rabbit leg from Bogan's fingers.

"Easy," Bogan cautioned, but the man tore the flesh from the bone as a wild animal would.

"I'd whup a hound of mine that wolfed like that," Conerley said disgustedly.

"You wouldn't let him get that hungry," Bogan said reasonably. "And where you keeping this big fat hound, anyhow?"

"Man, you ain't just foolin'. Our eatin' problem is gettin' real particular."

"Weather's too hot," Bogan said. "The game is making siesta from sunup till sundown."

"Be different in the States, won't it, Jess?" Beau Conerley asked in a voice that belied his own toughness, revealed his dependence on the tall man.

"Different?" Bogan said with a smile. "Kid, we're going to see the day when it's just too damn boring to eat another T-bone steak."

Conerley laughed aloud, his eyes shining brightly.

9

"Just wait and see," Bogan assured him. "You'll say to the waitress, 'Ma'am, ain't there a place in San Francisco where a rich fella like me can get some nice boiled jackrabbit?'"

Conerley laughed again, sank his strong teeth into the gamey meat without even tasting it. The man across the way, meanwhile, had looked up sharply at the first mention of the States, taken an intense interest in the conversation. It caused him to look at the other two more closely, and what he saw of Jess Bogan was size—taller than most men by a head—whose rugged, deep-tanned handsomeness had somehow preserved its amiability despite a broken nose, a knife scar along the cheekbone and what must have been a lifetime of battering and brawling. He placed Bogan's age at thirty, possibly less, and guessed that the threadbare clothing on his back now was all the man owned.

He put down the redheaded, freckled Beau Conerley as younger—twenty-five—and hardly tested by life if the other one was the yardstick. There was a wildness in this one, a kind of virginity, and his emotions were bubbling on the surface. Conerley, at first glance, seemed an unworthy companion to the big man, but when one watched them closely he saw how their personalities meshed, how they formed a comradeship whose point counter-point could survive a great deal.

His covert inspection of them was abruptly interrupted when the tall one broke off the pleasant day-dreaming about the good times ahead in San Francisco and turned his gaze on him.

"We're pushing on, mister," Bogan said. "What are your plans?"

"I want to go with you."

"The hell with *that*," Conerley said. "Patch you up and feed you, okay. But, by God, I don't travel with any man that would—"

"You have got to help me," the man said directly to Bogan. "I don't know where I am, but I must get out of this country!"

"Why?" Bogan asked simply.

The man looked away from that steady scrutiny, stared

into the ground. With his eyes averted he said, "I'm under sentence of death by the Mexican government."

It was spoken rather dramatically, but the words had little visible effect on his listeners.

"What'd you steal?" Beau Conerley asked. The man's head came up sharply.

"I didn't steal anything," he protested, then looked to Bogan again. "My name is Smith," he said. "Cyril Smith. I was—I am—a major in the British Army."

"Which is it?"

"All right, I'll tell you," Smith said impulsively, as if almost glad to bare an unpleasant secret. "I was stationed in India during the uprising," he went on swiftly. "God, if you think your redmen here are fierce you should fight against the Sikh devils. They're positively barbarous, without mercy." He paused for a breath. "My garrison was cut off," he said. "Completely surrounded by those fiends. I did the only thing possible. I surrendered." The man's head shook slowly back and forth at the memories he was evoking. "Back in London they saw it differently. I was recalled after the uprising had been put down and cashiered. My elder brother suggested it was best that I leave England for good, take up a new life over here."

"What happened?"

"I tried the cattle trade for a while," Smith said. "But that didn't work out. Your countrymen seemed to resent me. I was trying my luck on this side of the border when the war broke out. War," he said in a firmer voice, "is something I know about. I offered my services to the Mexican Army. They gave me command of a regiment. Irregulars." He shook his head again. "I never saw such a motley crew in my life. A collection of farmers, convicts, bandits—not a decent soldier in the lot."

"Sounds like you got licked," Conerley remarked.

"We were attacked by one of Taylor's main forces at San Jacinto. It was a rout. We never had a chance. My so-called regiment fled before them."

"How about you?" Bogan asked.

"What else could I do? I escaped then in order to fight again another day."

"But the Mex government wants to shoot you."

11

"The Governor had to have a scapegoat, didn't he? What better than an Englishman?"

"How'd you give 'em the slip?" Conerley asked him.

"I was under house arrest," Smith answered. "I got away during the night. It must have been a week ago. God, what a wild country this is!"

"House arrest?" Bogan said. "Isn't that when you give them your word to stay put and they don't lock you up?"

"Word!" the other man scoffed. "What does a Mexican know about a code of honor? And should I have let them kill me for the cowardice of their own soldiers?"

Bogan said nothing, showed nothing in his face, but he was thinking that if everything the man said was taken at full value then he was glad that the judgment was not in the hands of Jess Bogan. He turned to his partner.

"What do you say, Beau?"

"You're the one he nearly killed last night," Conerley replied. "If he goes along it's your say-so."

"You fit to travel, Smith?"

"Point the way for me," Smith said. "I'll make it somehow."

Bogan nodded. "We're due east of Mexicali at present," he explained. "Our destination is Holtville, in the States, and we've been trying to get there, so far, by avoiding any Mex towns along the way."

"You seem to be escaping the government yourselves," Smith said slyly.

"I used the word 'avoiding', Smith. There's some difference."

Smith shrugged his thin shoulders. "Care to tell me why your're *avoiding* Mexicans?"

"No, he don't care to tell you," Beau Conerley broke in sharply. "And, mister, don't try to find out. It'll cost you."

Smith looked from one face to the other, and what he saw in both of them convinced him that Conerley's threat was no idle one. Whatever their reasons were for staying clear of the Mexicans, they would kill him for learning them.

Camp was broken without further talk and the three of them set out on foot across the wild country, keeping the ascendant sun on their right, their faces pointed north. Bogan still retained the Englishman's service revolver, and his other armament was a holstered Colt and a carbine that looked weightless and small in his huge hand. Conerley, in addition to the formidable greener, wore on his left hip a shortened-barreled Remington in a cutaway holster that identified him as a gunman by trade. Skill and care had gone into that rig, hours and hours spent for the single purpose of gaining a split second's advantage at the showdown. There were a dozen-odd warriors with more natural talent that Beau possessed, men of reputation as fighters who now had all eternity to rue the infinitesimal fraction of time they had lost drawing against the redhead.

But if Conerley gave full notice of his profession, what then was Jess Bogan? To any lawman or inquiring magistrate the big man described himself—candidly and with no loss of pride—as a drifter. Pinned down, he would admit to pushing beef, to riding gun guard, hiring out in cattle wars and even one hectic winter as paymaster and peace officer for a brawling, Oregon lumber camp. Nothing to be ashamed of there, nothing dishonorable if judged by the morals of his time, but all in all the life of a tramp, a restless man wandering from his West Texas birthplace to the Canadian border, learning French from the girls in New Orleans, Spanish from their sisters in Tijuana. Nothing to be ashamed of, and nothing to show for it but memories.

Why, then, this careful avoidance of the Mexican authorities? Because he feared for his life? That was no reason at all in Bogan's case, a man who had good reason to consider himself on borrowed time for the last ten years.

The truth was that he and Conerley wanted more than just to keep out of Mexican hands. They preferred not to be observed at all in this land—and the reason was inside a leather pouch tied to a thong around Bogan's middle. That pouch contained nearly eight ounces of tiny, glittering metallic-tasting grains—grains that might be as worthless as so much sand—or precious as gold. A whole mountain of gold that a half-crazed old man had described to them a year ago in an El Paso bar. The old man wouldn't go

13

back there himself—just thinking about it set his body to trembling—but he told them vaguely where it was and bid them welcome to the hazardous journey. Where he was going was to Holtville, in California, to finish out his life there with a married daughter. And now Bogan and Conerley were bound for the same town, to have it assayed in the old man's presence, to give him his third share—and then figure out some way to make a deal with the hostile Mexican government to go back to the mountain and mine their millions. That is, if the stuff in Bogan's pouch was not so much worthless sand.

That was why they wanted to steer clear of Mexicans at this time. That was why Cyril Smith's or any other intruder's life was in peril if he suspected they had made a fabulous strike. They were not going to be like one Luke Freeman, the hapless sourdough who had been the first discoverer of gold in California—and profited not at all while other thousands made their bonanza.

Jess, as a matter of fact, was thinking of Smith right now, watching the man carefully as it became more evident with each passing minute that he couldn't keep up.

"A rest, Beau," Bogan said and saw the dark look Conerley threw Smith. They moved into the sparse shade of some scrub pines and Smith sank to the ground in complete exhaustion.

"Well, Jess?" Conerley asked. "What do we do with him?"

Bogan rubbed sweat from his eyes. "He'll make it," he said.

"Like hell he will. He's so close to dying I can almost smell it."

"He doesn't want to die, Beau."

Conerley stared down at the wasted figure on the ground. "Once I had a horse that busted his leg," he said slowly. "He didn't want to die either. But he had to." As he spoke his left hand came to rest on the jutting butt of the Remington.

"Once I had a horse that busted his leg," Bogan said, eyeing that hand. "My dad got him sound again. Took some patience, Beau, but I rode that horse *again*."

"You mean it, Jess? Healed a broken leg?"

14

GUNS OF REVENGE

"Took plenty of savvy."

"I'll be damned," Beau said and Bogan smiled inwardly. Conerley's hand was off the gunbutt, trouble was postponed, and he doubted if the little lie would count against him.

"How about we build him a litter?" Jess suggested, taking full advantage of his friend's new train of thought.

"Yeh, sure. Hell, he don't weigh more'n a bird. Tote him easy."

So they fashioned a crude stretcher, and though Beau was right about Smith's weight he was wrong about the ease of carrying him beneath the midsummer, sub-tropic sun. At ten o'clock in the morning it was one-hundred and forty degrees in that wasteland. No trees now, no water, nothing to do but push on while the breezeless, lung-scorching heat grew hotter and hotter.

It was not humanly possible to get used to such weather, but they did endure it, just as they had been enduring it for the past fifteen days. Days. That had been Bogan's decision, to make the trek by day, when no Mexican in his right mind would be abroad, when he kept to the dark coolness of his home. To make camp at dusk, stay low, and forage for their food when the game, such as it was, ventured forth for its own livelihood. They ate the white meat of rattlesnakes, telling each other how much it tasted like capon; and rabbit; and even dined on a Gila monster one night, without finding anything in civilization to quite compare it with. Only once had they found water suitable to drink, and for that vital stuff they either tapped the cactus plants or sucked moisture from the bitter red berries that grew everywhere.

But if it had been hard going for the past fifteen days, this sixteenth was draining even Bogan's reserve. Thirty minutes was the most they could bear the litter, and they would set it down, lie on the baked ground themselves, panting for air, not even speaking because of the precious energy it wasted. Then Bogan would push himself to his feet after five minutes, squeeze Conerley's sweat-soaked shoulder with a reassurance he hardly felt himself, and they would lift their burden again, move north at the painful rate of two miles every thirty hellish minutes.

15

Until, at two o'clock in that seemingly endless afternoon, Beau Conerley's knees sagged beneath him and the front end of the litter fell from his gripless fingers. He sat there on his haunches, pale blue eyes round and staring, the pupils reduced to pinpoints from the relentless glare of the sun.

Bogan lowered his end of the litter to the ground, walked on leaden feet to his friend.

"All the way down, Beau," he said, the words coming flat and uneven from his parched throat. "I'll hold your legs up."

Conerley's head moved from side to side.

"No," he said, his own voice a weak sound. "Gonna do it. Got to." His cracked, swollen lips continued to move but for several seconds he could produce no speech. ". . . him or me," Jess heard indistinctly through his own weary mind. "Can't—can't carry him—any more . . ." Beau struggled to a standing position, feet planted wide to support him, and to Jess it was like a dream to see Conerley lift the gun from its holster.

"Don't, Beau," he said to him. "Don't do it. We'll make it. . . ."

"We won't." He aimed the gun at the prone, long-sleeping form on the stretcher, found he had to hold it with both hands. Even so it wavered. Then, from the southeast, came a sound.

"Listen!" Bogan cried in a voice that was nearly his own.

Conerley turned his head with an effort.

"What?" he asked thickly.

"Didn't you hear it? *Thunder,* Beau. Thunder!"

"Lying, Jess," Conerley said. "Like you lied about that horse. Can't fix a busted leg." He swung back to Smith again, steadied the gun.

"Count, Beau," Bogan said. "Count to ten."

"Wha' for?"

"So you'll hear it. The thunder."

Conerley shook his head, then suddenly halted the movement. He had heard it, too. The low, low rumbling thunder. He turned partway around, looked to the southeast. Overhead loomed a cloudless, merciless blue sky with a huge

16

white disc in its center. But in that direction the sky was dark, menacing-looking.

"Count," Jess Bogan said again. "Count the time. One," he said then, persuadingly. "Two. Three . . ."

Conerley didn't join in the count but his head nodded with each number that Bogan intoned.

". . . Eight—" Another peal of thunder, and just before it a streak of jagged lightning. "It's closer, Beau, closer!" Bogan told him. "Count the seconds!"

Now both their voices blended. "One. Two. Three . . ."

At "three" they saw the lightning, at "six" they heard the thunder. And all at once the sun was blotted out, a great, cool breeze engulfed them. There was moisture in the onrushing air, they could smell it, taste it. A bolt of lightning crashed not a hundred yards away, thunder rolled over them, and the sky, for as far as the eye could see, was black.

And, man, how it rained. A cloudburst that emptied a fantastic two inches of moisture onto that water-starved land in the next twenty minutes.

Both men swept their hats off, inverted them on the ground to catch the precious water. It was then that Bogan discovered he was holding his Colt in his hand, though he couldn't remember drawing it. Did it mean that he'd planned to stop Beau from shooting Smith? There was no clear answer in his mind—and all that mattered was that it hadn't come to pass. . . .

He suddenly burst into laughter at Beau, who was whooping and hollering in the downpour like a kid on a holiday. Then his partner began stripping off his shirt, unfastening his trousers, and in a matter of moments was capering around in the buff.

Bogan sat down, laughing all the harder, fell over on his back and just lay there with his mouth open wide to catch the delicious stuff and let it trickle down his throat.

The man on the litter awoke with a start, stared all around him, fearfully until he remembered where he was. He raised himself on an elbow, and so ludicrous was the sight of Conerley snake-dancing in the rain that even Smith could forget his troubles and enjoy a smile.

For twenty minutes the rain fell, and then stopped as

17

abruptly as it had begun. The black clouds raced on to the northwest, the sun came out, and so thirstily had the cracked earth drunk in the water that within five minutes it was as though it had never rained at all.

"Help yourself to a drink, Smitty," Bogan heard Beau Conerley say and looked on in wonder as the redhead tilted his hatful of water toward the lips of the man he'd so nearly killed half an hour earlier.

"Thanks, chum," the Englishman said gratefully, his voice stronger-sounding.

"Sure you had enough?"

"Plenty. And if you'll give me a hand up I think we can dispense with this bloody stretcher." Beau reached down and helped him to his feet. "Must have been some ruddy go, hauling me along like that."

"Wasn't so bad," Beau said airily, then caught Bogan watching him and gave his sheepish grin. No man lived more in the present than Conerley. No man that Bogan had ever known could turn his back so completely on the past if the past was not to his liking.

"Let's get going," Jess suggested, hoping to take full advantage of the new vitality in all three of them. They still had to walk slow, to accommodate Smith, but they didn't have to stop again until a solid hour had passed. Now the sun was to their left, and though the air was still ovenlike, there was less discomfort.

"Where do you figure we are, Jess?" Beau asked.

"Close," Bogan said. "Pretty soon now we'll start cutting westerly. That's when the fun might start."

"Fun?" Smith asked. "How do you mean?"

"We came down here by way of Yuma," Jess told him. "There seemed to be some difference of opinion as to who owned what. I'm not too sure they've got it ironed out yet."

'They' didn't. The war with Mexico was over. Technically there was peace between the countries, and in far off Washington D.C. they were remaking the maps, penciling in a new border. But right here there was no peace, no agreement at all. The land still in dispute was some forty miles deep, an area that seemed to belong to everybody and to nobody at the same time.

GUNS OF REVENGE

The greater part of the Mexican Army, so badly mauled by Taylor, had fled back into Lower California. But there were smaller groups who fought on, as guerrillas, as bandits, bitter men who had once lived in this land now being claimed by Americans as U.S. soil. It was a time of great confusion and strife, and when Jess Bogan said that now the fun might start he meant that the three of them were right in the middle of Nobody's Territory.

"How far to Holtville, Jess?" Conerley asked.

"Can't be more than fifteen, twenty miles. Figure about three to four more hours travel."

"Wouldn't it be safer to do this last stretch by night?" Smith suggested.

"We've had our best luck by day," Jess said. "It's the night that brings out the Mex troops."

"Troops?" Smith asked.

"Well, whatever they are. A kind of ragtag army that won't quit fighting."

"Got a great fondness for hangin' prisoners," Beau Conerley put in conversationally. "Which don't bother me none so long as I'm pullin' the right end of the rope."

Smith's hand went involuntarily to his thin neck.

"Maybe it is safer to travel by day," he agreed.

"Jess'll spare us a necktie party if any man can," Conerley said, getting up from his resting place. "Well, boys, what say? We can put in another hour and a half before sundown."

They began the trek again and Jess led them in a direction that was slightly west by north. And now there were signs of civilization—adobe buildings scattered haphazardly over the countryside, fields that showed indications of cultivation before being abandoned, dried skulls of cattle. In the distance they even saw two figures mounted on burros.

"Give you ten thousand cash for that mule, *amigo*," Beau said wistfully. "Make it twenty-five for the span, on the barrel-head."

"Spending a lot of money," Smith said jokingly.

"Hell, a drop in the bucket to what Jess and me—"

A glance from Bogan had stopped him in mid-sentence. He clamped his lips in a tight line. Smith looked at him,

19

then at Bogan, and his own face grew thoughtful. They walked on without further conversation, came to a final halt for the day when the sun was an orange globe poised on the horizon.

"Food ain't going to be such a problem tonight," Jess said then. "Just have me a blaze going when I get back." He left them, returned less than thirty minutes later with two wrung-necked chickens in tow, a look of mischief on his face. Beau took one plump bird from his hand, held it aloft and gazed at it as if Bogan had brought back the Czar's crown.

"Man!" he said. "Man, oh, man!"

"Has anything ever looked so good?" Smith asked.

Bogan laughed. "Took me back to my sprattin' days," he said with a strange shyness. "Breakin' into somebody's coop."

"How'd you find 'em, Jess?"

"I heard the cock raising hell about something a way's back. I tell you, my mouth's been watering ever since."

He and Conerley dressed the fowl then, sectioned it and cooked it over the fire. They stopped feasting only when there was nothing left but bare bones, topped off the meal with cigarettes from Bogan's near-empty pouch, and sat facing each other in quiet contentment.

"Jess," Beau Conerley said unexpectedly, "the day I threw in with you I picked a winner."

"Mutual, kid."

"How long have you two been together?" Smith asked.

"Must be two years. Right, Jess?"

"Ran into each other in Dodge," Bogan told the Englishman. "A thousand miles from the Big Bend, and it turns out we were born only five miles apart."

"I was in that part of Texas, myself," Smith said. "Pretty hard country."

"Hard and poor, Smitty," Conerley told him. "Awful poor."

"You'll go back someday, Beau," Bogan said. "And so will I."

"Let's go back together, Jess. In high style." He slapped his thigh happily. "Man, we'll be forking the two slickest ponies in West Texas and toss silver dollars in the

20

street . . ." Once again he caught himself saying too much and fell silent. Bogan smiled, tolerantly, looked over at Smith.

"What plans you got?" he asked him.

The man laughed harshly. "Plans," he echoed. "All I know is soldiering."

"Maybe another war'll turn up for you," Beau said cheerfully. "I remember before we left Yuma there was a lot of talk about California settin' itself up independent. That ought to heat up a nice argument."

"I heard that, too," Smith said. "Fremont's army. It all came to nothing."

"Well, something'll turn up," Beau repeated. "It nearly always does—" He broke off speaking as Bogan came suddenly and swiftly to his feet. "What's up, Jess?" he whispered.

"We got company out there," Bogan told him quietly. "I heard a horse." He moved into the shadows, bent his head.

"Better douse the fire," Beau said, standing near him.

"No. Go back and sit down with Smith. Keep talking naturally, but have your gun in your hand." He slipped the Englishman's revolver from his waist. "Give him this," he said.

"What are you gonna do?"

"Circle back, see what the proposition is. Be set to break for it if I give you the word." He moved away then, was lost to sight seconds later, and proceeded at a right-angle to the direction whence he had heard the horse whinny. A hundred feet later he cut back in again, moving for all his size with the stealth and silence of a cat.

He could hear the voices of Beau and Smith rather clearly, make out the dim light of the fire. Then, between himself and the camp, came another voice—low-pitched, speaking Mex.

"Deja aqui los caballos," it said. Leave the horses here.

"Quien es?" asked another.

"Yanquis."

"Bueno, bueno!" said still a third voice, younger and excited.

At least three then, Bogan thought, hearing them dis-

21

mount in the pitch blackness. He counted out five seconds, moved forward quickly and came upon their horses. Three horses. Now he stalked the men, very slowly, making allowance for the fact that they would pause outside the camp and take count of their own quarry. A silhouette took form not ten feet ahead—the outline of a wide sombrero, thick shoulders. His sharp eyes scanned right and left, located the other two advancing toward the firelight at six foot intervals.

"Baja," the one in the center grunted and they all three went down on their bellies, began to inch forward. The leader lifted his arm and they stopped.

Bogan could see what the Mexicans could—Beau and the Englishman sitting crosslegged near the fire. Except that his left hand was not in sight, Conerley appeared natural and at ease. But Smith kept darting anxious glances toward the darkness.

"Mire!" said the voice of the young Mex. *"El Ingles!"*

"Callese!" the leader growled. "I can see for myself it is the damned coward."

"El General will want to see him, too," the third man said.

"Hay mas?" the leader asked. "Are there more? Do you see any others?"

"No."

"Cuidado ahora—careful now. We want the dogs alive, but watch yourselves." With that they rose to a crouching position, rifles held close to their bodies, and crossed boldly into the camp.

Beau Conerley had spotted them half a minute before. "Expect visitors, Smitty," he said in an undertone. "Stay loose."

"Mexicans?"

"Yeh."

"They'll kill us."

"Jess is behind 'em. Let him call the play."

"But suppose he isn't. . . ?"

"Just stay loose."

The Mexicans broke upon them, three ferocious-looking, hot-eyed fanatics whose appearance spelled out no nonsense.

GUNS OF REVENGE

"Rendiran!" shouted the leader. "Surrender! Throw up your hands!" The rifle in his hands jerked upward to illustrate the command. Conerley responded promptly. Smith hesitated.

"Suba! Up!"

"He means business," Beau said out of the side of his mouth. "For crissake get 'em up." Smith's hand came away from the gun hidden under his leg and he raised both of them to the level of his shoulders.

"Los registra," the leader said. "Search them." And as the other two moved toward the seated pair Jess Bogan stepped from his watching place, closed with the leader and jabbed the barrel of his Colt into the small of the man's back with the same motion that he locked the Mexican's neck in the crook of his huge elbow.

"Alto!" he ordered sharply. "Hold it. *Abajo con los fusils!"* That one dropped his rifle, as much to keep from being strangled as anything else. The other two whirled in their tracks, startled, frozen with uncertainty. Then a gun roared at their backs. Again. Again. Four times in all, jerking each man's body in turn, pitching him face down into the ground.

The gun blasts reverberated, then all sound passed away leaving a weird silence in its wake. Bogan and the man in his grip and Conerley were gazing fixedly at Smith, each wondering what he planned next with the smoking gun in his hand.

Bogan let go of the remaining Mexican, stalked over to where Smith sat.

"What the hell gives with you, mister?" he asked seethingly, outrage naked in his face. "What in the name of God made you so trigger-happy?"

"I saved your life," the Englishman answered self-righteously. "Another second and they would have shot—" Before Bogan could stop him Smith suddenly raised the gun again, fired past him twice. Bogan spun around, saw the leader of the little raiding party sink to his knees, hands pressed to his chest, an expression of vast surprise on his dying face. Bogan's arm swept out, caught Smith flush on the cheek and sent him reeling backwards. Still raging, the big man jerked him to his feet, cocked a tremendous fist.

23

"Easy, Jess, easy!" Beau Conerley shouted. Bogan stayed the blow, looked into his partner's face. What he saw there puzzled him.

"You don't think he did right, Beau?"

Conerley shrugged. "Those boys were some rattled," he said. "Who's to say for sure what they might have done?"

"And that one?" Bogan asked, hooking a thumb over his shoulder.

"I wasn't watchin'."

"He made a move for the rifle," Smith said groggily. "I gave him what they had planned for us."

"He's got a strong point there, Jess," Conerley said.

Bogan stared down into Smith's face. "Who's *El General?*" he asked, seeing the quick alarm appear there.

"Ortega?" Smith murmured worriedly. "They're with him?"

"They thought he'd be glad to see *el Ingles* again. How come, Smith?"

"General Ortega commanded the army I was attached to. It was his orders that sent me on that suicide mission to San Jacinto." As he spoke, the Englishman's voice grew indignant. "A general," he sneered. "The man was a butcher. Do you know what he's called? *El Lupo.* Absolutely no concern for human life. . . ."

"You hold it pretty cheap yourself," Bogan told him.

"And I say I saved yours. Not that I expect your gratitude. . . ."

"Last night was the only time I was in trouble," Bogan reminded him dangerously. "You want my gratitude for that?"

"I was out of my head, Bogan. I've been meaning all day to tell you how sorry I feel about that."

"Listen, boys," Conerley interrupted. "We made a considerable ruckus just now. If these three got company out there. . . ."

"You're right, Beau," Bogan told him. "Let's hope those horses didn't spook off."

"We got horses?" Beau asked eagerly, following Jess into the darkness. "You mean I'm gonna *ride?*"

The animals showed their training, having stayed put where their late riders had dismounted.

24

GUNS OF REVENGE

"Man, oh, man," Beau Conerley said affectionately, running his hand along the withers of a young sorrel filly. "Oh, you sweet little thing. You darlin'—Oh, oh," he said suddenly. "You hear that, Jess?"

"I heard. Let's go." He led two horses back to the grisly-looking camp, tossed the reins of one to Smith, scooped up his carbine and swung lithely to the saddle. "They're coming hard," he said.

"Ortega?"

"It sounds like a big party."

Smith scrambled furiously aboard his horse. "We've got to get away!" he shouted. "I can't let that fiend get his hands on me again!"

Bogan brushed past the man contemptuously, led the way out of there, giving the spirited animal its head, relying on it completely to put them on a trail.

"Can't we go faster?" Smith shouted.

"You take the lead, mister," Jess invited.

"No. But Ortega's men are vaqueros. They ride like the wind, and they all come from around this country. . . ."

"You didn't rate 'em so good at San Jacinto," Bogan reminded him.

"These are Ortega's personal troops. Handpicked—"

A burst of fire cut him off. Bogan's horse, as if used to that sound at his rear, laid his ears back and broke into the most graceful galloping stride Bogan had ever experienced. No wonder this Ortega's men rode like the wind. A second fusillade sounded and the marvelous horse lengthened its stride even more, as if it could judge the distance of the pursuing riders.

"Man, oh, man!"

Beau was just off his shoulder, roaring his joy, heedless of any danger behind them.

"Oh, you flyin' little darlin'!"

The filly, responding to the rich praise, decided to show the human what she could really do. In an instant she was abreast of Bogan's stallion, straining to pass him. But the stallion liked it up front, drew on some reserve he'd been saving and surged ahead.

"Come on, baby, come on!" Beau urged her. And she gave him more speed, held herself neck-and-neck for

25

another fifty yards. But then the bigger horse drew ahead. Half a length, a length—and it seemed to Bogan that the longer the lead became the faster the horse ran.

"Jess, up ahead there!" Beau shouted to him and both men had apparently seen the string of campfires at the same moment. A mile away, Bogan guessed, and threw a look over his shoulder. He could neither hear nor see any more shooting, and if pursuit had really stopped then the next logical guess was that the campfires belonged to an American patrol, that Ortega either couldn't or wouldn't engage them tonight.

Bogan tightened the rein, kept the stallion galloping but not at that breakneck pace.

"What do you think, Jess?"

"I think we might have made it, boy. Did you ever have such a ride?"

"Well, you just wait till this little girl's a year older. We'll race you another time. . . ."

"Are those Yankee lights?" Cyril Smith asked shrilly. "Are they?"

"Could be, Smith," Jess answered, anger and scorn for the man reignited by the sight of him. *"Adios."*

"What do you mean?"

"I mean so long, good-bye. This is where the trail splits."

"I was hoping we might ride together for a bit," Smith protested. "At least until we reached Holtville."

"What business do you have in Holtville?"

"That's just it. I have no business anywhere. And no funds," he added plaintively.

"Hell, ride along," Beau invited. "What's the difference, Jess?"

"This morning you wanted no part of him," Jess said. "Tonight I don't. We better get together on Mr. Smith, one way or the other." He pressured the stallion's ribs with his knees, put the horse out ahead and rode alone.

"He'll get over it, Smitty," Conerley told the Englishman confidently. "He's never stayed sore more than fifteen minutes in his whole life."

"Sort of leads you around, though, doesn't he?"

"The hell you say! Jess and I're partners. Fifty-fifty, right down the stack."

"Oh, I suppose you divide the spoils," Smith said, watching the younger man's face closely. "But I've noticed that your large friend makes all the decisions."

"Well, you noticed wrong. You're still along, ain't you? Whose decision was that?"

"Only because you put your foot down, Beau. You asserted your own personality for once—and let me tell you, it was a fine thing to see. I was proud of you."

Beau sat a little straighter in the saddle. "Stick around, Smitty," he said. "You'll be seeing a lot more of it when we hit Holtville."

"What's there, anyhow?"

"Old gaffer name of Arnett. We're in with him on a— We want to talk to him," Conerley finished.

Up ahead, Jess was halted by two sentries.

"State your name and your business, civilian," one told him gruffly.

"Jess Bogan, soldier. Enroute to Holtville."

"Where you comin' from?"

"Down south aways."

"Meet any guerrillas?"

"Just ran away from a pack."

"How many?"

"Couldn't tell exactly."

Smith and Conerley rode up. The other sentry approached them, began the same questioning.

"You two boys can pass through. We're taking the Englishman to the Lieutenant."

"What for?" Beau asked.

"Don't ask questions, cowboy. Just ride on."

"And don't give orders, soljerboy," Beau replied with his quick heat. "That fella's a friend of mine and I'm vouchin' for him. . . ."

"Come on, Beau."

"Leggo, Jess. Just cause Smitty wasn't born here these soljers figure to push him around."

"Nobody's pushing anybody around," the sentry growled. "I got orders to hold all foreigners for the

27

Lieutenant. That's what he is by his own admission and I'm holding him."

"Well, you can hold me, too. . . ."

"Beau, will you come on?"

"And you can quit pushin', too, Jess. I'm makin' my own damn decisions from now on. You wanna walk out on a guy when he needs help, you go ahead and do it. Me, I'm stayin'."

Bogan looked from his friend's stormy face to catch the smile on Smith's. Someone was rocking the boat, Jess realized, and if Beau could be maneuvered this easily he could just as easily be made to part with their discovery in Mexico.

"We'll both stay, Beau," he said. "You hold one of Smitty's hands and I'll hold the other. Wonder to me how he lived this long without us."

Escorted by the sentry they made their way into the camp, identified by a guidon at the headquarters tent as being A Company, 5th Cavalry Regiment. Conerley, looking a little defiant about the whole thing, went along to the tent with Smith and the soldier. Bogan took the chestnut stallion to where A Company's big-chested mounts were strung out, got permission to water his horse from the corporal on duty.

"Feed him, too, if he's hungry, fella."

"Well, much obliged."

"Looks like a runnin' horse," the corporal said sagely. "Where'd you get 'im?"

"I found him," Jess said.

The corporal nodded. "Just so the owner don't find you," he said.

"The owner's dead. Tell me, who is Ortega?"

"We been chasin' El Lupo for two months," the soldier told him, "but I'm damned if we ever see him. There's some kind of invisible line, what they call the New International Border. So long as El Lupo stays on his side we can't so much as spit at him. But if we catch him on this side we can hang him." The soldier smiled. "Except that nobody is sure where this invisible border is, and that makes it a funny game. You didn't appropriate that horse from Ortega, did you?"

28

GUNS OF REVENGE

"From one of his boys. Ortega's riding around just five or six miles from here, in case you're interested."

"The Lieutenant might be. Then again, he might not. There's some rumor going round that if you make the mistake of getting yourself kilt on the south side of the invisible line then your poor widder can go whistle for your pension." He smiled again. "So the Lieutenant he wants to be damn sure which country he's in when El Lupo castrates him, if you know what I mean."

"Makes me relieved I'm a civilian," Jess said.

"Ah, this life ain't all bad. There's a lot of discontent at the moment, what with so many not wantin' that long march back to New Orleans. Me, I enlisted for another seven years."

"When do you go back to New Orleans?"

"Regiments are leavin' every day, seems like. Gonna leave a small force in the Territory till the civilians organize their own law and order. You want a drink?"

"Wouldn't mind one at all."

"Ain't got any here," the corporal said. "But you head down that way, toward number three platoon bivouac. There'll be a skinny private playing a mouth organ, and most likely a crap game. You tell any soldier there that Hanks sent you."

"Bring you back something, Hanks?"

The corporal shook his head. "Lieutenant's a good man," he said. "But he's hell on drinkin' when you got the duty. Enjoy yourself, cowboy."

"Sure obliged," Jess said. "Me and the horse."

He followed directions, and sure enough the strains of a harmonica came to him, and the click of dice, and the same rough language of soldiers carousing as it was in Caesar's army. Number three platoon had made a clearing for itself, a kind of open-air gaming area, and Bogan stood off, watching them at their recreation with not a little envy. Many and many a lonely night he had wondered about the military life, weighed his situation at that particular time with the companionship, the security, the travel of the soldiering man. But something had always come up.

He stood off, watching them, but Bogan was not built to go unnoticed. The soldier who spotted him, in fact, was

29

cut from the same general mold—six-feet-plus, two-hundred-plus, with a leathery face, close-cropped hair and three yellow chevrons on his light blue summer blouse.

"Step up, puncher," the sergeant bellowed congenially. "The game's wide open!"

Bogan shook his head, turned his pants pockets inside out to show how empty they were.

"Drinks are free," the other big man invited. "Help yourself, citizen."

Bogan grinned in anticipation, strode forward to the jug in high spirits. Four months, he was thinking. What would it taste like? Another sergeant was holding the jug and he eyed the smiling Bogan warily before surrendering it, then had his suspicions confirmed as Jess hefted it expertly on a cocked elbow and let the fiery stuff flow freely. Sixty seconds went by and the assembled troopers gazed in awe at the performance.

"You've seen it all now, boys," the sergeant bawled raucously. "A damn, hollow-legged, drink-forever Texan!"

Bogan finally lowered the jug, wiped his hand across his mouth.

"Sure cuts the dust fine," he said, passing it back. The sergeant came up to him, long arm extended.

"Put 'er there, buddy! They call me Bronco!"

An unreformed muleskinner, Jess thought, liking the feel of a hand he could grasp rather than envelop.

"I'm Bogan," he said.

"Texas?"

"Big Bend."

"Well, I mighta knowed! You all of you drink down there like it was the last call before kingdom come! Waco's my home, Brother Bogan!"

And Bronco spoke as though he were trying to be heard in Waco.

The harmonica player stepped forward, a lean soldier with deep-sunken eyes and a dead-serious expression.

"Orv Yunker's my name," he said. "Owensboro, Kentucky. Challenge you here and now to a johnny-go-round."

There was an immediate roar of approval. Two stoppered jugs appeared like magic.

"I bet five on Texas!"

30

GUNS OF REVENGE

"You're took! And five more on Kaintuck!"

"Old Yunk weaned on sourmash!"

"The Texan's bigger!"

"Put your money where your mouth is!"

The money came out, a profusion of greenbacks and silver from these soldiers who had no place to spend their pay, nothing to do with it but gamble. Gamble on absolutely anything.

Bogan saw the money, saw the excitement in their faces. He held his arm aloft, signaled for silence.

"Boys," he said, "I couldn't out-drink a Baptist deacon. Not tonight. . . ."

His audience shouted its disbelief. One voice, from a tiny, baby-faced private, rose above the rest.

"Up Texas!" the recruit cried out. "Strike another blow for liberty!"

Bogan laughed with the rest, kept shaking his head.

"You got the spirit, kid," he said directly to the boy. "Step out here and proxy me against this Kentucky champion."

"I don't drink!" the boy yelled.

"Me neither," Bogan yelled back. "Not tonight."

Catcalls followed that. Hoots of derision. Then his fellow-Texan, Bronco from Waco, threw an arm around Jess' shoulder, raised the other one with a fist at the end of it.

"He don't want no damn contest!" the sergeant thundered at them. "But let all them that would like to fist fight with my friend Bogan form a line right here! Come on, lads, here's your chance!"

There were no takers, but the idea of it diverted their leap-frogging minds from the johnny-go-round and they were happy again. But in every crowd there is one man with an idea. In this crowd it was someone named Leach, a private not conspicuous in the 5th Regiment for his derring-do.

"Box the cowboy your ownself," Leach bawled. "Give us an exhibition, Bronco."

The drinking bout had been a fine proposition. But this suggestion really caught their fancy. They seemed to have a taste for battle.

31

"No, no, no," Bronco protested grandly. "A professional like myself can't indulge himself for pleasure."

"For profit then," said Leach, tossing a silver dollar at the ground beneath Bronco's feet. "We'll make a purse, and winner take all!"

Other dollars followed, paper and silver, and within seconds there was a respectable pile.

"Take it back, boys, it wouldn't be a contest." He stood back from Bogan, cuffed him familiarly, belittlingly on the back of the neck. "Right, Bogan?"

Jess had ducked the drinking contest for the very good reason that there is never a winner. Only two losers. But the cavalryman's easy assurance of taking him with fists was something else again. And the little cuffing, though not at all painful, was a goad.

"Right, Bogan?" the sergeant yelled in his ear again, and it seemed to Jess that the man was demanding a spoken answer.

"Right, Bronco," he told him. "But work yourself into shape and I'll give you a try at me." Jess was grinning as he spoke and now he returned the sergeant's cuff with something extra added.

Bronco winced, pushed his square jaw forward.

"Come again, laddiebuck? I'm not in shape, says you?"

"Don't blame yourself, Sarge. It's the soft life."

Bronco began getting white around the lips as his gorge rose. The men of the platoon sent out a steady stream of encouragement.

"Square off with 'im, Bronco!"

"Twist his mug around!"

"Loosen his teeth for 'im!"

The sergeant stepped back, sucked his belly in and began slowly unbuttoning his blouse. "I promise you a fair, professional fight, Bogan," he said. "I don't bite, gouge or kick."

"I'll try to remember," Jess answered, peeling off his worn cotton shirt. He felt good, exhilarated, and the weariness of a whole day spent walking seemed to be lifted.

The two big men faced each other, and if there had been a rough similarity about them before there was none now. Bogan's midsection was as flat as a board, not layered with

32

the tire of fat that hung over Bronco's belt. The muscles in his arms and sloping shoulders lay smooth beneath the tanned flesh, weren't bulging and knotted like the other man's.

Bronco brought his arms up in the approved fashion, assumed the classic boxing stance, and though Jess understood that was the way the experts fought he also thought it was awkward and ineffective. He felt more at ease with his feet closer together and both hands about level with his ribs. There was not much defense to it, but in the brawler's way of thinking the best defense in a fight was how often and how hard you hit the opposition.

"Are the boxers ready?" demanded Leach, the self-appointed referee.

"Ready," said Bronco.

"Ready," said Bogan.

"Fight!"

Bronco laid a jab flush against Bogan's mouth, did it three more times in succession as Jess slowly circled around him. Bogan took it a fifth time, patiently waiting for his man to commit his right hand. Bronco did, swung it ponderously in hopes of finishing the crude amateur with the one punch. Instead, the fist passed harmlessly through the air as Bogan slipped under it and buried his own hard hand to the wrist in Bronco's ample belly. A terrible groan sounded and the soldier doubled over. Bogan's left smashed into Bronco's nose, like a man chopping kindling, and then he hit him again in the middle. Bronco went down, which is a disastrous thing if the rules are to be followed. For now Jess could stand over him, club him back down every time he tried to rise, and unlike a saloon fight, Bronco had no recourse to his feet or a chair for protection.

But Jess either forgot this important advantage, or thought he didn't need it, for he stepped back and waited, licked away the blood from his mouth. Bronco climbed slowly to his feet, looking sick, and very methodically assumed the cumbersome stance that had been his undoing a minute before. And Bogan resumed his circling tactic, exposing his face, willing to take the stiff jabs in exchange for another clean shot at that inviting middle. But Bronco very much didn't want to get hit there again—not by this

33

strong boy. As a result he dropped his arm cautiously low when Bogan aimed a blow for the stomach—a blow that suddenly changed direction, arched upwards and caught the boxer full in the jaw. Bronco was hit almost simultaneously on the other side of his face, and then the man was just standing there, rocking to and fro, eyes glassy. Jess stepped backward, measuring him, and delivered the merciful finisher. The brawler stood looking down at the professional, remembering half a hundred fights that had been so much tougher, wondering if he had inadverently violated some special code of honor.

It was not a popular victory—Bronco was the Third Platoon's champion—but the cowboy had fought fair and they bore him no animosity as they dragged the sergeant to the water trough. The jug of white corn was produced, and when Bogan unhooked his lip from his teeth he took a long, soul-satisfying pull, handed it back and put on his shirt again.

"Here's your purse," Leach said and Jess took a single silver dollar from the pile, grinning lopsidedly.

"For luck," he said and started back to his horse.

"Get your drink all right?" Corporal Hanks asked.

"Sure did. Fine bunch of boys."

"Say, what happened to your mug?"

"Nothing much," Bogan said, taking the horse's reins back over his head, swinging into the saddle. "Thanks for everything, Corporal."

"See you again."

Jess rode toward the HQ tent, in front of which the other two horses were still tethered, and as he waited he wondered if perhaps Smith had run into some kind of trouble with the military. He had little knowledge of the laws and regulations pertaining to foreigners, except that he had heard of some hardcase up Oregon way being accompanied across the border by vigilantes and told to stay in Canada or else.

And wouldn't that be something—if the U.S. Army tossed Smith back into Mexico? After all the damn trouble they'd been through with the murdering little bastard, that would really be something. Except that his pal El Lupo would pick him up, and there would be justice of a kind in that.

Then Smith and Conerley walked out of the tent, along with a young lieutenant, and Smith was smoking a long cigar. They shook hands all around and the lieutenant went back inside.

"Guess what Smitty's gonna do, Jess," Beau said when he was in the saddle again.

"What?"

"He's gonna join up with the Territorial Army of California," Beau said admiringly. "The Lieutenant give him a letter to some colonel up to Westmorland. The Lieutenant says they'll give him an officer's commission for sure."

Bogan looked at Smith, who was puffing on the big cigar and smiling importantly.

"Hope you don't have the same old trouble with this army," he said quietly.

"What trouble?"

"The trouble you had in India, then again at San Jacinto."

"I don't know what you're trying to imply, Bogan, but I don't think I like it." He had stopped smiling. Bogan wheeled his horse around.

"Coming, Beau?"

"We're both goin'," Beau said.

"I thought Smith was going to Westmorland."

"It's on the way."

"The hell it is. Westmorland's north of here. Holtville is due west a couple of miles."

"They call America a free country," the Englishman said tartly. "That means I'm free to travel where I please."

"Why the big interest in Holtville?"

"Ah, come off it, Jess," Beau complained. "Stop ranklin' about three dead Mexicans. Let bygones be bygones."

Bogan put his horse on the westerly trail, set it at a steady trot without another word. But he was thinking. He was thinking that if Smith pushed his nose any further in the business of Jess Bogan, then Smith would be a dead man.

T W O

They called it Holtville now, which had a Yankee sound to it, but for a hundred years it had been a Mexican settlement, and as Jess Bogan turned into the dusty, narrow main street it seemed that he might just as well be in Calexico, El Centro or Araz Junto. It was small and haphazard, its buildings were predominantly adobe brick—and except for the small saloon, Holtville was sound asleep at nine o'clock of this sultry evening.

Bogan reined in before the saloon, hitched the stallion to the rack and was entering the place as Conerley and Smith pulled up. He had had the hope, on the road from the bivouac, that Beau would pull abreast of him, that they would talk over the Englishman and the advisability of shaking him out of their lives *muy pronto*. But Beau had chosen to ride with his new friend—the fellow he had had in his gunsights twice within the past twenty-four hours—and the necessary powwow had to be deferred.

Jess pushed the swinging doors aside, stepped through and stood for a moment surveying the assortment of faces at the bar and the tables inside the smoky, whisky-scented room. And they were an assortment, some twenty of them, ranging from a smooth-faced youngster who stood drinking with half a dozen men of Bogan's own age and general appearance; a well-dressed man of Beau's age who sat in a corner with two young and pretty Mexican girls; the usual gathering of older men who either kept to themselves or played cards.

Twenty faces in Holtville, but none of them belonging to old Branch Arnett, and as Jess moved forward toward the bartender the two following him entered the place.

"What'll it be, son?" the round-faced, thick mustachioed man behind the bar asked.

"Some bourbon and some information," Jess said. The drink was poured as Beau and Smith crowded in beside him.

36

GUNS OF REVENGE

"Ask for room," a man next to Smith said with a kind of quiet menace, "and maybe you'll get some. Otherwise," he added, bunching his hand on Smith's shirt and pulling him backwards, "don't shove your way in."

Bogan considered the advice reasonable and paid no more attention. His interest was in the bartender.

"I'm looking for Branch Arnett," he said in a low voice. "Where can I find him?"

"Haven't seen the old man for a week or more," the barman said, glancing meanwhile at Smith, trying to gauge the chances for any real trouble to erupt.

"Where does he live?"

"He's staying with his son-in-law, Frank Washen. Their ranch is about two-three miles north, right on the road to Sandia—"

Beau Conerley's voice broke over the barman's, each word clipped and clear, metallic-sounding. Jess knew that special tone well, knew that the redhead's reckless anger was working in him.

"How about me, bud?" Beau said. "Am I in your way?"

"Not yet you're not."

"And if you ease down some, you think there'll be room for my friend?"

"Maybe," the other man said. "If your friend asks me."

"I couldn't be bothered," Smith put in snappishly.

"Suit yourself," the man said, putting his back to both of them and resuming a conversation on his left. All that, thought Jess Bogan, was reasonable on his part. Beau didn't.

"Make room," he ordered, the voice a notch tighter to Jess' ear. The other fellow turned his head, unhurriedly, gave Conerley a level gaze.

"This ain't your dunghill, friend," he said—a warning that was clear to the attentive Bogan—"so mind your manners."

But Conerley didn't size up the situation, didn't realize that these six at the bar were a group, all of them armed and stamped capable. Either that or his temper was in full charge.

"I'll tell you to make room one more time," Beau said. "After that, mister, defend yourself."

The ultimatum caused a stirring among the man's companions, sent them fanning out calmly into a half-circle that closed Beau inside.

"All right," the man said. "Tell me one more time."

There was a pause then, a moment of utter silence that extended throughout that tense, frightened room, and in that tiny fragment of time Bogan moved—casually, almost boredly, but now his tall frame blocked his friend from all their guns. He looked at none of the six, spoke directly to Smith.

"There's room at the other end," he said. "If you came in here for a drink, get it there. If you didn't, get out."

There was utter gratefulness in the Englishman's face as he moved out of that death zone under Bogan's protection. He went where he was told with neither a word nor a backward glance.

Now Bogan could meet the gaze of the gunmen ringed around him, look neutrally into each one's eyes and shift to them the responsibility for whatever happened next. *Now it's up to you,* his expression said. *And if it's a fight, you've got two of us to handle now.*

"Friend, I'd like to buy you a drink," said the man whom Smith had crowded originally, and the sound in his voice broke the awful tension.

"Friend, I'd be obliged," Jess told him. "The name's Bogan."

"I'm Riker," he said, "and these days extra partial to peacemakers." Jess could see the strain and fatigue in the man's lean, beard-stubbled face. It was a gray look.

"Trouble?" Jess asked, and Riker smiled wearily.

"I've seen four friends killed this month," he said in a monotone. "I've watched forty acres of grass scorched black, found a hundred head of prize stock with their throats cut."

"That's not trouble, mister, that's war."

"Yeh," Riker said, staring into the liquor in his shot glass. "That's war." He tossed it off with a single swallow. "What's your line of work, Bogan?" he asked then.

"Pretty mild, compared to yours," Jess said. "Right now me and Conerley here are looking up a friend."

"Hope you find him," Riker said. "We rode up tonight

38

to pick up a shipment of new rifles. Naturally," he added, "the Spread Eagle luck continues lousy. The soldier boys won't release 'em."

"How come?"

"They call it contraband, I call it politics. God knows what Ben Barthen will do when I go back down and tell him."

"He the bossman?"

"Yeh. And I wish to hell he'd of stayed put in Arizona. Either that or held off till the damn border was settled."

"Who's your trouble with?"

"They call him El Lupo," Riker said. "He was a general during the war, and I'm damned if I know how we won it. One tough, smart, Mexican sonofabitch, believe me."

Bogan looked puzzled. "We met the army east of here," he said. "They're chasing him, too."

Riker smiled again. "They're chasing their own tails," he said bitterly. "Lupo cuts off a small bunch, has them make some noise. The army takes off after 'em, and Lupo hits us."

All this while Jess had been waiting for Beau to take some part, but the redhead stood stiff and silent, pouring steadily from his bottle. It was time to get Conerley away from here.

"I wish you luck, Riker," he said, "and thanks for the drink."

"Obliged to you for stopping a needless fight," Riker said. Beau swung around.

"Don't be so sure it's stopped," he threatened. "I'd like to meet you head-to-head."

Riker sighed. "You look like you might be good, son," he told him, "and I wish I could accommodate you. But I just can't afford it."

"A new way to say yellow—" Beau only said part of that to Riker direct. During the rest he was being turned in Bogan's big hands and marched forcefully toward the doors, on out into the street.

"Jess, damnit, take your mitts offa me! By God, nobody manhandles Beau Conerley—"

"Ahh, Beau, for crissake give it a rest, will you?" Jess told him tiredly, releasing him.

39

"Don't ever lay a hand on me again, Jess. I'm telling you."

"And I'm telling you that when men are partners what the one does reflects on the other. And when a partner of mine gets out of line he's going to get slapped down. . . ." Conerley was backing away, body crouched, eyes boring into Bogan's face. "Now what, Beau?" Jess asked him softly. "You're going to throw down on me?"

Beau had stopped, legs planted wide, poised to draw. The sound of Bogan's voice died away. Slowly, Conerley's body relaxed, straightened to a natural position. He shook his head from side to side, in disbelief.

"God Almighty, Jessie, what's gotten into me?" he asked the big man plaintively. "What makes me so damn proddy?"

"You could probably do with some gentling, kid," Bogan told him goodnaturedly. "If there's a crib in this town go find it. I'll look up Arnett, meantime."

"There was a couple of likelies in there," Beau said. "Why don't we both lose the fine edge?"

"First I'll settle our business. You go on, Beau. Cut loose a little."

"A splendid idea," Cyril Smith said, stepping from the shadows where he had been an avid spectator to the near gunfight. "Come along, Beau. A frolic is very much in order."

"You don't need me with you, Jess?"

"No. Suppose we meet back here in a couple hours?"

"Fine," the Englishman said, including himself in their plans with bland assurance. Jess watched him walk off with Beau, close as his shadow. More like a leech, he thought, and getting more and more under my skin. He mounted his horse, rode out of Holtville toward the ranch of Frank Washen. Two miles or so, according to the bartender.

Bogan found the place with some difficulty, and found it seedy and rundown, overgrown with weeds, in emergency need of repair, all but vanquished by the merciless onslaught of nature in this lonely land. He remembered how glowingly the old man had described his son-in-law's thousand-head spread in "Californy," of the life of comfort and ease with which he would end his hard days. And this squat, squalid-looking adobe building must be the *"hacienda"* the old man had pictured for him back in El Paso.

And from the little house came the sound of a female voice, its words clear and coolly spoken.

"Whoever you are," it said, "just turn right around and go back where you came from."

And though Jess was on the wrong end of that command he found himself smiling a little at the confident authority with which it was given.

"I'm not bringing you any trouble, ma'am," Bogan answered. *Baroom!* went a shotgun, belching fire and fury, and a no-longer-smiling Jess Bogan threw himself flat in the dirt.

"You're darn well told you're not," the calm young voice assured him then. "Now pick yourself up and vamoose. I won't aim to miss with the second barrel."

"Listen, lady," Jess said, "I'm here on peaceful business. . . ."

"I've heard that before," came the swift reply. "Just get up and get out before I count three. One . . ."

"Business with Branch Arnett," Bogan put in.

"You got business with Gramps you bring it to him in broad daylight. Two . . ."

"Tell him Bogan's out here," Jess said. "The fella he talked with over in 'Paso. Tell him I just got back from that trip to Mexico."

"Mexico?" she echoed, and then laughed briefly, chiding him. "Not to hunt for that magic mountain full of gold?"

"Let me speak to Arnett," Jess said, beginning to wonder how the old man and anybody else in there could stay asleep through that shotgun blast and all this palaver.

"Describe him," she said unexpectedly.

"Do what?"

"If you really know my grandpa, then tell me what he looks like."

"Well," Bogan said, "he's a nice old geezer, about as high as my shirt pocket. Not big, but cocky as a bantam rooster. Showed me two words tattooed on the inside of his arm. Said they were Latin for 'truth' and 'freedom'. Anything else you want to know about him?"

41

"No, I guess you know Gramps all right," she admitted. "And you can get up off the ground, too."

"Well, thanks," Jess said dryly. "Do I also have your permission to talk to your grandfather?"

"He's not here," she said. "But don't get any ideas. I can take care of myself with or without help. . . ."

"Lady, I believe it. But where's Arnett?"

"Gone to work for the Spread Eagle," she said. "What did you want to tell him about the mountain?"

"Spread Eagle?" Jess said, frowning. "Where the— where's that located?"

"South," she said. "About ten miles. You didn't find any gold, did you? It was just another wild idea of Gramps', wasn't it?"

"What's he doing at Spread Eagle?" Jess asked, trying to get an answer to his problem.

"Fighting Mexicans," she said simply. "Spread Eagle sent a recruiter through the country, said he'd hire anybody to do anything. Gramps was kind of disappointed with the mess this place was in, anyhow. So he signed up for a year to try to get some money together."

"Signed up to fight Mexicans? That old man?"

"I guess he wanted to help somehow," she answered. "What with my father taking off and all."

"Taking off where?"

"Back east. He was an actor until he got sick. He got better out in this climate but he wasn't much at ranching." The girl laughed wryly in the semi-darkness. "Me neither," she added.

"You live here with your mother?" Bogan asked. There was a pause now.

"My mother passed away two months ago," she said quietly.

"Sorry to hear that," Jess said. "Does that mean you're living here all alone?"

"I have company," she said, the warning note back in her voice again. "This shotgun, a Greener and a Remington. All loaded," she added, "in case you're interested."

"Sis," Bogan said, "I'm not even curious. But what do you live on?"

"I have a job in town," she said. "I'm waitress at the

Holtville House. Now let's hear about Gramps' mountain. Did you find anything?"

"We brought back a sample," Jess said. "I want to get an assay and then make some kind of deal with your grandpa. Either sell the claim to somebody outright or figure a way to go back down there and mine it ourselves."

"You came all the way here?" she asked incredulously. "For Gramps?"

"It's his mountain, not mine," Bogan said simply. "We just went where he told us."

"We? You got somebody with you?"

"My partner's back in town," Jess said. "Seein' the bright lights."

"And you actually found gold?"

"I couldn't tell you what we found. I never mined for anything in my life. But what we got is awful heavy for its size, and it sure does glitter when you wash it off."

"Lordy!"

"Now don't get your hopes up. Even if it is gold there's still plenty of problems. The damn mountain—pardon the expression—but the mountain is still in Mexico. That don't make it easy to get any gold out."

"What did you say your name was?"

"Bogan."

"Just Bogan?"

"Jess Bogan."

"You sound sober, Bogan," she said then. "Are you?"

"You ask some funny questions," Jess told her. "Sure I'm sober. Why?"

"Well, I'm considering," she said. "I'm considering whether to invite you in for a cup of coffee. Just coffee. Or whether to send you packing."

"I'll help you with that big problem, ma'am," Bogan said, "and wish you a safe good night." He turned and started toward the hitchrail.

"But I'm so darned curious," he heard her say, as if speaking aloud to herself. "What does a man look like who'd come clear up here when he could have kept the mountain to himself?"

Looks right now like a plain damn fool, Bogan thought and swung lithely into the stirrups.

43

"Wait," she called to him. "You can have the coffee."

"Thanks, anyhow," Jess called back, "but I promised my ma never to take favors from strange women. She warned me about the pitfalls an unmarried fella faces in this world. . . ."

"Pitfalls?" she echoed, her voice outraged. "You certainly don't think I would. . .? Well, of all the brass!"

"Bachelor man can't be too careful," Jess said blandly. "Who knows what might be sneaked into his coffee cup when his head was turned?"

"Oh, you're just joshin', aren't you?" she said then, laughing. "Making fun of me."

"A mite," Jess admitted. "But you're right. This ain't no time of night to take a stranger in. When I see your granddad I'll tell him that you're taking fine care of yourself."

"If I wrote a note, would you take that to him, too?"

"Be glad to."

"Well, come on in, then. I'll write it while you're having your coffee."

Why not? Jess thought. She might even have some real coffee from a grinder, not those damn beans or chickory weed. He also admitted to some curiosity about seeing her face. Seeing if it went with that nice clear voice. . . .

He dismounted, looped the reins again and strolled toward the little house. The door was opened to him, and the flickering candlelight in the room beyond framed the shapely, medium-tall figure of the girl. Jess halted a foot short of the threshold and doffed his hat, stared down into her upturned face.

"Howdy-do," the big man said very formally, conscious of a constriction in his chest, a quickening of his pulse. Lord Almighty, she was the most beautiful-looking thing he'd ever laid eyes on. Beauty with strength, built to last, to ride out any storm.

"Come in, Jess Bogan," she said, and so full of his own confusion was Jess that he failed entirely to note the quickening in her voice, the mutual attraction she shared.

He stepped past her, gingerly, shyly, as if almost afraid to make even the slightest physical contact.

"Lordy," she said, "but you're a high one."

44

Jess nodded. He, too, was acutely conscious of his size.

"Enough for two men and some left over," she said, then laughed. "I don't see now how I missed hitting you out there," she told him.

"I'm an easy target," he agreed, his manner serious.

"And easy*going*, I hope," she said. "I'd hate to think of you being mad at anyone." She smiled.

It suddenly got through to Jess that he was being flirted with, in a roundabout way, and he grinned at her.

"I ought to be mad at somebody," he said, "for making me eat dirt a few minutes ago."

She held out her hand, impulsively. "I mistook you for a tomcat from Holtville," she said. "They seem to come prowling around here when the firewater puts ideas in their heads."

Bogan took the soft warm hand in his own, didn't dare to grip it. She left it against his palm.

"Well?" she asked then. "Aren't you going to ask me my name?"

"What is it?"

"Mary," she answered. "Plain and simple."

Not hardly, Bogan thought, and she read it in his eyes, withdrew her hand.

"Sit yourself down and be comfortable," she said. "I have water boiling for my tub, so the coffee won't be but two minutes." She swung away, walked briskly from the sitting room to the kitchen. Bogan took a restless turn of the room, stopped by a table to examine a gilt-framed monograph of a very handsome man in a black leotard and ermine-collared cape. His head was erect and his eyes seemed to pierce right into Bogan's mind. The resemblance to Mary was astonishing, and Jess read the two inscriptions. The first, in white lettering, read: *'Mr. Franklin Washen as Hamlet, Prince of Denmark, The Mayfair Theatre, Boston, July 18, 1840.'* The second, in a flourishing longhand: *'For Both My Beloved Mary's—From Their Adoring Husband And Father.'*

Jess tried to stare back into the face in the portrait, tried to establish a man-to-man understanding, form a tolerance for whatever it was that had prodded the actor to run out on his 'Beloved Mary's'. Too much pride? He'd

45

been sick and gotten well again. But he was no rancher. So he'd abandoned this rough life to get back to something he knew. But it was going to be rough *getting* back to it, Jess decided, and he decided to leave his womenfolk with at least a roof over their heads while he made himself a new stake at acting. Then he was going to send for them, when he was a big success on the stage again, all togged-out in fancy costumes and people applauding in the theatre. That was it, Bogan decided. It had to be. That girl out there in the kitchen hadn't been handed any fly-by-night of an old man. . . .

Mary came through the doorway at that moment, carrying a steaming mug of coffee. She smiled at him again, for no reason, set the mug down on a table beside a comfortable-looking easy chair.

"Bad news," she said.

"What's that?"

"I was *sure* I had milk, but I haven't. You'll have to sip it black and strong."

"Always do," Jess said. "And I ought to take it in the kitchen, not out here."

"There wouldn't be room left for you in there," Mary said, smiling. "I've got the tub in the middle of the floor and my nightgown hanging over the stove."

Jess looked at the lovely girl over the rim of the mug and wished she would quit talking about her bath and nightgowns and such. He had been a long time on that mountain, a long time on the trail getting back here. And he was a natural man.

"Of course, if you'd rather go into the kitchen. . . ."

"No," Jess said. "No, this is fine. And real good coffee, Mary."

"Thank you, sir," she said, curtseying playfully.

"You did that," Bogan laughed, "like an actress. You going to be one, too?"

She shrugged her slim shoulders, and sighed. "I don't know what I want to do," she said. "I guess I better decide on something soon."

"Yeah," Jess said, laughing again. "You're getting on in years."

She nodded solemnly, her blue eyes serious. "I'm nineteen," she said.

"Another year," Jess said, "and you'll be a regular old spinster lady."

"With my shotgun for company," Mary said and they smiled into each other's eyes for a long moment. "What," she asked him then, "does a fellow like you do? I mean, what plans do you have?"

"A fella like me," Jess said carefully, "doesn't plan beyond tomorrow. Oh, sometimes he's set for the day after. What you call a drifter."

"Sounds like a good life."

"Well, I don't know if it's a good life or a bad one," Jess said. "But it's the only one I can tolerate."

"Can't settle down in any one place?"

Jess grinned. "I could," he told her, "except for one thing."

"What's that?"

"I'd keep wondering about the other place," he said, finding that in talking to her he was explaining something to himself. "Which is kind of loco, actually."

"Loco? Why?"

Jess shook his head. "Because down deep," he said, "I don't much care for traveling all the time. A part of me wants to sink roots somewhere, and a part of me is restless to see all there is to see." He suddenly looked startled, smiled self-consciously at himself. "Who wound my clock, anyhow?" he asked, draining the coffee and getting to his feet again.

"There's more," Mary said, but Jess held up his hand.

"If you'll write that note to your grampa," he said, "I'll be gettin' along. . ."

There was a knock on the door, a kind of signaling rap, and they both turned that way.

"Miss Mary? You all right in there?" a voice called inside. She went to the door and opened it, revealing a young, loose-jointed cowboy in the doorway. His glance went to Bogan's face and there was suspicion in it.

"Hank, what are you doing here this time of night?" Mary asked him.

"Runnin' an errand for Mr. Riker," the cowboy told the girl but still looking steadily at Jess. "He asked me to check your place on the way out. See if everything was all right." The way the youngster spoke the last it was plain that in his mind everything here was not all right.

"That was thoughtful of Fran," Mary said. "Hank, this is Jess Bogan. A friend of my grandfather's."

Jess nodded cordially but the tough young ranny kept scowling.

"I seen him in town," he said. "Him and his proddy sidekick."

"You sound," Jess said, "like something's bothering you."

"Maybe something's gonna be botherin' you," came the surly answer. Or somebody . . ."

"Hank!" Mary said. "What kind of talk is that?"

"Well, would Mr. Riker like to find this gunswift here?" Hank said. "And where'd he ever meet your gramps?"

Bogan stepped forward. "Sonny," he said easily, "why don't you finish running that errand and let other folks mind their own business?"

"Because Mr. Riker's my foreman and Miss Mary's his girl. That makes it my business!"

"I am not his girl!" Mary protested.

"He thinks you are," the youngster said sharply, "and that's good enough for me."

"Well, it's not good enough for me," she told him. "And when I see Mr. Fran Riker I'm going to have a talk with him about it."

Hank looked surprised and saddened by her words.

"You like Mr. Riker, don't you?" he asked, his voice a lot different.

"He's a fine man and we're good friends," Mary answered. "But I'm not his or anybody else's *girl.*"

"I'd appreciate it," Hank said then, "if you wouldn't speak to him about it. Not and mention me, that is."

"I won't, Hank. Providing you stop riding around the countryside carrying tales about me and Fran Riker."

"I won't speak another word on the subject," he agreed. He should have made his good-bye then and left. Instead he stood stolidly in the doorway and glared at Bogan. Jess regarded him thoughtfully for a moment, then looked down at the pretty girl and smiled.

"I'd better leave," he said. "I think this fellow's getting ready to call you my girl."

"No such a thing," Hank said. "But your leaving Miss Mary's house is a good idea . . ."

"This is none of your business, Hank," Mary said angrily, "You ought to be ashamed!"

"Or have his mind scrubbed," Jess said lightly. "So long, Mary, I'll give your regards to your granddad."

"You don't have to go, Jess," she said. "I'm not worried about any gossip . . ."

"Nor ever will be, I'm thinking," Bogan told her. He put his hand on Hank Plover's bony shoulder. "You've got some growing up to do, bucko," he said without malice. "I hope you make it."

Jess rode back into Holtville in a troubled frame of mind. If he shut his eyes he had a clear picture of the girl before him. Her oval face and deep blue eyes, her long hair unpinned and the color of old gold, her supple young figure and graceful movements. He smiled briefly as he recalled that for all her complete femininity she could speak her thoughts and handle a shotgun fine.

But then he wondered if he'd done right in mentioning the sample from the mountain. He should have been very vague with her, not giving her the slightest hope that there might be good times ahead. Coupled with that was a foreboding about following Branch Arnett to this Spread Eagle outfit. That was big trouble down there, somebody else's trouble, and Bogan was sure he could run into enough grief of his own without chasing after it like a damned fool.

But since he did have to discuss business with the old man the thing to do was to be absolutely set and determined, to swear a solemn oath that nothing or nobody would detain him there five minutes after his business was settled.

In that stubborn mood he arrived back at the saloon, found the man Riker still there with his party but no sign of Beau and Smith. He looked at Riker and thought of Mary Washen again. She was not his girl. Jess had heard

49

her say that in so many words. She wasn't anybody's girl.

Riker nodded to him cordially, indicated that there was room beside him, and Jess went to the bar again almost reluctantly.

"We were just talking about you, Bogan," Riker said. "I want you to meet these boys." He named each of the five in turn, each man nodded to his name, and Jess deliberately kept his mind a blank. He didn't want to know their names, remember their faces, drink their whisky or have even the slightest tie to them.

Riker was pouring a generous tumblerful of the redeye into Jess' glass as he spoke to him.

"We were talking about you and wondering how you'd like the best paying job in the Territory," the foreman said. "I got a notion that you and Spread Eagle would be fine for each other. . . ."

Jess, without realizing how violent he looked, slammed an outsize fist on the mahogany top and set glasses and bottles clattering the whole length of the bar.

"No!" he said in a loud, clear voice. "Not on your life!"

"Easy, man, easy," Riker said plainly startled. "What are you so riled about?"

"I'm not riled, damnit. I just don't want any offers." As Jess spoke his voice grew steadily calmer, and there was a halfsheepish expression on his face at the relization of how vehement he must have seemed. But these boys just didn't understand. They didn't have his chance to strike it rich. Their lives and their loyalties were pledged to the man who owned Spread Eagle.

"Well," Riker said easily, "I'll withdraw the offer. How's that?"

"That's fine," Jess said, grinning his relief.

"And instead I'll ask you point-blank for help. One man, Bogan, to another."

The grin disappeared. Jess looked, in fact, almost as pained as Sergeant Bronco had after that belly blow.

"Now listen, Riker," he said. "You ain't got no call to put things on a personal basis—"

"Just say 'Yes, I'll help out,' or 'No, you can go to hell.' Texan, aren't you?"

"What's that got to do with anything?"

"Nothing," Riker said, looking the big man steadily in the eye. "Well, Bogan, which way do you answer, a Texas man to a Wyoming man?"

Wyoming, Jess thought miserably. How many of those cold country scudders had he ridden with? This Riker was a sonofabitch for hitting a man where he lived. He took a pull of the whisky.

"Now listen," he began again, a little desperately. "The sad fact is I have to ride down to your outfit on some personal business. . . ."

"Well, fine!" Riker said. "That settles it." He lifted the bottle at his elbow and refilled Bogan's glass.

"Damnit, that settles nothing!" Bogan protested. "I got something important going for me!"

"What's more important than giving a hand to your friends when they're hurting?"

"Where do you get that stuff, anyhow? I walked in here an hour ago and you and me were total strangers. Why, hell, brother, we came within an ace of killing each other —" Jess broke off. Riker was smiling at him, so were the others. He was hooked and they all knew it. The foreman held out his hand. Bogan took it glumly, sealed the deal.

"You and me, boy," Riker said, "are goin' to be hell on wheels. You know that?"

"I know I got roped into something that could cost me my big chance."

Riker laughed, slapped him warmly on the back. Then he looked past Jess, his glance caught by the returning Hank Plover who was motioning to him.

"Be right with you, Bogan," Riker said and strolled off. Jess watched the errand boy's animated conversation, the obvious references to himself. Riker sent Plover away, returned to the bar with an expression that was definitely cooler.

"Understand we might have some mutual friends around here," the other man said.

Jess smiled. "That's a fine young fella you got on the payroll," he said. "I hope you don't let him eat with the men."

"Never mind Hank," Fran Riker said. "I'd like to know

51

what you were doing out at the Washen place tonight."

"Well," Jess said slowly, "if that's a friendly request for information I might tell you a part of it. But if it's anything else, mister, I'm afraid you're going to have to go to hell."

Riker made a grimace of his mouth as he considered the answer. Then his eyes mellowed slightly. "All right— it's a friendly request. What were you doing out at my girl's house this time of night?"

"Well," Jess said as before, "I don't know now if I was. What does this roped and branded yearling look like?"

Riker's jaw jutted forward. "Were you at Mary's place tonight or not?" he demanded.

"That was the name she introduced herself by," Jess admitted. "And the lady also made it pretty clear that she had no liens or attachments."

"Oh, she did, did she?"

"Crossed the t's and dotted the i's."

Riker scowled menacingly and Jess straightened up a fraction from his lounging position against the bar.

"Where'd you know the lady before?" Riker said, making an effort to control his voice.

"Never saw her in my life," Jess said. "But it could get to be a real nice habit."

"And you just happened to be riding out that way? First ten minutes in Holtville and you head straight as a birddog for the Washen ranch?"

"I had directions from the barkeep here," Jess said. "Ain't that right, buddy?"

The bartender, shaking with his nervousness, nodded his head. "You asked for the Frank Washen ranch," he said timidly, "and I told you. I swear, Mr. Riker, I had no idea . . ."

"*Frank* Washen?" Riker said to Jess. "You know her dad?"

Jess shook his head. "I know her mother's dad, Branch Arnett. I was told to look him up at his son-in-law's place. His granddaughter, this unattached filly, said I could find him down to the Spread Eagle."

"Oh, *well*," Riker said, smiling his relief. "Why didn't you say so in the first place?"

Bogan smiled right back at him. "Then she asked me in for a cup of coffee," he said mischievously. "I tried to beg off," Jess added. "But . . ." His voice dropped away and he shrugged man-to-man fashion.

"But what?" Riker asked.

"But I like coffee," Jess said. "Don't you?"

"The things I like, Texas," Riker said, "don't belong to another man."

"Amen," Jess said and turned away from the bar.

"Where you going?"

"To get a little air."

"You coming back?"

"Sure."

"And you're riding with us?"

"You and me shook hands on it, didn't we?"

Riker looked at Bogan, seemed to smile in spite of himself.

"We shook," he agreed. "Should've known better than to ask, Bogan."

"Thanks, Riker," Jess said and walked out of the saloon. He hadn't gotten a hundred feet of his aimless, restless sightseeing when a hand touched his arm and he looked down to see a girl's pretty face. She was one of the two Mex girls who had been sitting at the table back there.

"Hola, guapo," she said in a soft, pleasing voice.

"Hi, honey."

"No hable espanol?"

Her smile was sparkling bright and infectious.

"Poco mas o menos," Jess said. More or less.

"Tu me gusta," she told him with an easy familiarity. *"Un hombre grande."* Him she liked. He was so big.

Jess liked her, too. The smile, the liquid brown eyes, the thin cotton blouse that just about contained her straining bosom. A natural man, he reminded himself for the second time this night. And it had been such a long time since he had known a woman's sweet comforting warmth.

"Quiere dar un paseo?" she asked. "Do you want to take a walk?"

53

A walk, Jess thought. Down by the riverside. Or maybe she had a dark little room off one of these sidestreets. It would be hello and good-bye and no regrets.

Bogan shook his head gently.

"Yo no puedo," he said. "I can't."

"Porque?"

Why? That was a good question. Why couldn't he? He smiled at himself, at his own foolishness, when he thought of the answer. He couldn't because he was promised—promised to a girl he was never going to see again.

"Come on, *querido,"* the pretty little Mexican urged in Spanish. "Take a walk with me. We'll have a good time. *Muy mucho."*

"No we wouldn't, honey," Jess answered in English. "I've got to walk alone."

She didn't understand the words but there was no mistaking the meaning. She shrugged her shoulders, turned and went on her way.

2

Beau Conerley and the Englishman were waiting for him when he got back, sitting glumly at a table in the corner.

"Where the hell you been?" Beau asked with some irritation. "We got here an hour ago."

"Went for a little walk," Jess answered. "You make out satisfactory?"

"In this nine o'clock town? We damn near got tossed in the pokey for just talkin' to a couple of girls."

"That's tough, Beau."

"Yeh, tough. What're you feelin' so frisky about?"

"Frisky?" Jess echoed. That was exactly how he did feel, rejuvenated. But he didn't realize it showed on the outside, too.

"You must have—ah—transacted your business," Smith suggested.

"Did you see Arnett?" Beau asked.

"No," Jess said, glancing at Smith briefly. "He took a job with a cattle ranch south of here. We can look him up there."

"What do you say, Texas?" Riker called from the bar. "We better pull out."

Bogan nodded to him.

"What's he talkin' about, Jess?"

"They work the same ranch Arnett's at," he explained. "I sort of told him I'd throw in for a while."

"What about me?"

"You're not committed, kid. That Riker backed me into a corner. . . ."

"They payin' gun wages?"

"We are," Riker said, coming to stand beside Bogan. "Hundred a month and found."

"No cowpunchin'?"

"Everybody helps where he's needed at Spread Eagle." Conerley shook his head. "Not for me, mister."

"Ranching too hard on you?" Riker asked him.

"All that's for hire is this," Beau said, patting the holstered Remington. "It fights for your beef, mister, but it don't work it."

"All right," Riker said. "I'll sign on the gun." He turned to Cyril Smith. "What's your specialty?"

"I'm a soldier, sir," Smith answered crisply.

"He's bound for Westmorland," Bogan added pointedly. "Going to join the army."

"Spread Eagle could use a soldier," Riker mused.

"It could indeed," Smith assured him. "I fought with General Ortega. I know the man's every tactic."

"Is that so?" Riker said, impressed.

"And nothing would pleasure me more," Smith said, "than to fight against El Lupo."

"Come on along then. Ben Barthen will want to hear your ideas on that bastard."

They rode out of Holtville, nine of them, and Bogan was beginning to think that he had somehow inherited the damn Englishman.

3

Ben Barthen was a small, black-bearded man, but if he lacked physical stature it was more than made up for by the size of his ambition, the driving energy that led him on and on in a seemingly unquenchable desire for wealth and position. The owner of Spread Eagle, a vast and sprawling ranch whose headquarters was in Arizona, was an Easterner by birth—a Jersey Stater who had run away from a quarreling, unhappy home at the age of thirteen and made his own way ever since. When the boy reached Kansas he stopped running, found work with an English cattle brokers firm, running errands at first, then being promoted to the job of tallying beef as it came off the trail and into the pens.

Both his own employers and his employers' customers found Barthen to be a bright, quick-minded youngster of scrupulous honesty and devotion to his work. The drovers, cheated in so many of their dealing with the buyers, came in time to take Ben Barthen's count of their stock as beyond suspicion and unarguable. It was almost as if he were a third party to the transaction, present for the sole purpose of a fair deal all around.

When he was seventeen years old he was moved inside the brokerage office, given a desk and another phase of the intricate business. He stopped thinking of cattle as animals, saw them as figures in books, dollars and cents and pounds sterling. But if he had been able to protect the cattlemen as a counter, there was nothing he could do to prevent their being swindled in the actual buying and selling. His firm, which pretended to operate for a nominal ten per cent commission, ended up with much, much more than that by the time a herd was finally disposed of. They took, in effect, a commission from everyone they dealt with—the drover, the slaughterhouse, the tannery— and though the young man appreciated business acumen, he also realized that a firm that took such outsize profits was open to competition by someone willing to work for less.

But he had no capital, no connections, and so he had to bide his time. That time came when he was twenty-one and his firm made him a cattle buyer, sent him on long trips into Texas, Oklahoma, Wyoming, Arizona, allowed him to negotiate on their behalf to contract for beef. Barthen had with him large sums of money, in the form of sight drafts, and he made it a point not to keep these on his person any longer than possible, nor to store them in hotel safes where he stayed. Instead, he deposited them upon arrival in a cattletown with the local bank, used the deposit to acquaint himself with the bank's principal officer. He knew that these were the men who kept the cattle business going, good times and bad, and that the money he carried with him represented the liquidation of the notes they carried with the ranchers.

He made a good impression on the bankers, indicated to them that although he was a buyer his sympathies, like theirs, was with the man who raised the beef. And it was to them that he first suggested a Co-operative, an organization financed by a network of small town banks that would work in practical partnership with the ranchers, be at the same time both the seller and buyer. The net result, of course, was to be the elimination of the firm he was then representing—and he moved very slowly. It was, in fact, some five years later before he handed in his resignation at the brokerage. His direct boss was shocked, couldn't believe that a man of Barthen's talents could throw away his career just as he stood on the threshold of success. All the way from New York City came the General Manager, a pompous Englishman, who demanded that the resignation be withdrawn. Barthen thanked them and politely smiled his refusal. Six months later the company got the real blow. Something called the Cattleman's League, with offices in Dallas, had stolen nearly eighty per cent of their suppliers.

Ben Barthen put in ten more years as the guiding hand of the far-ranging co-op, grew progressively rich from it, but the more he roamed the cattle country the more he yearned to be a cattle baron himself.

The chance came in the year of the Panic, 1837, when cattle prices zoomed to an all time low. That financial crisis, coupled with a year-long drought and a disastrous winter, sent a staggering number of ranchers under. Barthen, for a ridiculous figure, picked up fifty thousand acres in Arizona that he named Spread Eagle. As his luck would have it, the Panic subsided, the drought ended, and the demand for beef and leather became overwhelming. Spread Eagle prospered, year-in, year-out, did it so effortlessly that its owner became restive for something new, something more challenging. Then the war with Mexico erupted and Spread Eagle became an important source of close supply for Taylor's army. He took trips into the battlefields, talked to the field commanders, got a firsthand knowledge of the military and political maneuverings. He also took a professional look at the land in dispute, saw how a man with nerve and imagination could take advantage of the chaos that would follow the peace. Then he moved, moved five thousand head of beef across the Colorado River and claimed for Spread Eagle ten square miles of graze west of Yuma and northeast of Mexicali.

In the center of that rich land lay the Rancho del Ortega, a truly splendid, luxurious ranch that featured a magnificent Moorish *hacienda* of fifty rooms. It had been abandoned when its owner took up arms to fight for Mexico, the same General Ortega who was now called El Lupo. Barthen and Ortega were now locked in a private war of their own for its possession, a war that El Lupo was waging with ruthless passion and guile, that he was winning with guerrilla tactics designed to exhaust his enemy's resources on one hand, terrorize him on the other.

Barthen had crossed the Colorado with five thousand head and fifty punchers to work them. Ortega's fierce vaqueros had cut the size of the herd in half, killed twenty of the cowboys outright and seriously wounded another twelve. Spread Eagle had scoured the land for help—gunfighters, especially—but even with men trained for combat, Ortega's raiders were prevailing.

But Barthen still held the *hacienda,* he still had the good right arm of Fran Riker, and last month his son Carl had come from the East to join him—along with Carl's bride, a pretty, unabashedly flirtatious girl named Miriam.

Ben Barthen's own marriage had not been a success. Life in this wild country had been too much for his wife to endure and she had returned to New York with their son when the boy was six. Ben had provided amply for their comfort, kept in touch via an annual letter and never forgot birthdays and anniversaries. But a year ago, during the terrible influenza epidemic that spread along the eastern seaboard, his estranged wife had died and Ben sent word to his son to come west and join him. There had been a vague reply to that offer, neither a yes nor a no, and if Ben had studied the wording more carefully he might have discovered the trait of indecision that ran through young Carl Barthen's character.

He had grown up too much under his mother's influence, too dependent on her judgment in all matters, and though he was twenty-six years old when the woman passed away, Carl was like a rudderless ship. He had been engaged to be married at the time, to a young lady his mother had approved of, but naturally there was no thought of a wedding to follow so close on a funeral— and during that period Carl began to seek diversion in sections of New York that his mother would have frowned upon. He ate in Delmonico's and Gallagher's, whiled away the night hours in bars along Broadway and down in Greenwich Village, and was introduced to a girl named Miriam, who made a precarious living as a dancer in a chorus line and seemed remarkably alluring and glamorous to the impressionable young Carl.

He still continued to see his fiancee, of course, but his visits to her home on Murray Hill became more and more infrequent. And when the young lady's father asked him point-blank to set a date for the wedding, Carl shied off completely. He fled to Miriam's flat in the Village and proposed to her at two o'clock in the morning.

The dancer told him she was very fond of him, that he was as sweet as any boy she knew, but she wanted time to think it over. She'd just turned twenty, she pointed out, and her 'career', as she put it, was just starting. That next evening, when she reported for work at the cabaret, Miriam demanded of the owner to be taken out of the chorus line immediately and be given a solo number. The man not only refused but warned the girl that unless she reported on time she would not even have her job in the chorus. Miriam stomped out of his office, found Carl at the bar and suggested they elope right then and there.

They did, and spent a month in Atlantic City for a honeymoon, but when they returned to New York Carl's bank had an unpleasant bit of news for him. His account

59

was overdrawn five hundred dollars. He immediately wrote to his father for the money, and while awaiting a reply went in search of a job that befitted his genteel background and education. The best he found paid twelve dollars a week as a runner on Wall Street. Miriam tried to get work dancing but found that she had been blacklisted for quitting her previous job without the usual notice. Then they had to move from their spacious midtown flat to a small one on the lower East Side. And they had their first real quarrel when Carl came home from Wall Street to find Miriam entertaining some of her former girl friends and several well-dressed men who were complete strangers to Carl.

A week later a letter finally completed its rugged journey from the Mexican border country. In it was a draft from his father for a thousand dollars and a reminder of the invitation to join him at the ranch. Carl and Miriam talked about it at length, and when the extra five hundred was all but gone they decided to accept the offer and start west. The bridegroom was especially relieved because he was not at all certain that Miriam would stick with him if there wasn't plenty of money for her to spend.

The young couple arrived at the ranch six weeks later, and within forty-eight hours Ben Barthen saw that his daughter-in-law's presence was going to mean trouble. The clothes the pretty girl wore might be the latest thing in the East, but they were much too revealing for this part of the world. And Ben was frankly shocked at the things she discussed in mixed company, at the provocative glances and bold smiles she bestowed on every man on the place. He knew there would not be trouble from his own punchers, for Spread Eagle was their life, but he worried about the hardcase gunmen that Riker had taken on—rough, dangerous men who would have no conscience about Miriam just because she was the owner's daughter-in-law.

Barthen, on the night that Riker rode in with the three new recruits, had just about decided to send his son and his wife back to the home ranch in Arizona. There would be plenty for the shy, introspective Carl to do there—and God knew there was plenty about the ranch business his son had to learn. Why, he even rode like an Easterner—and the sight of a six-gun seemed to fill him with alarm. Barthen, in plain truth, was not pleased with the man his son had become.

He was also not pleased when he saw Riker's party enter the flagstone courtyard without the shipment of new rifles they were supposed to escort from Holtville. He was so displeased that rather than wait for his ramrod to report to him, Barthen strode from the big house.

"What's wrong?" he said in a clipped voice, one long-used to giving commands. "Where are my guns?"

"They're there, Ben, four crates full," Riker said, dismounting wearily. "Army slapped an embargo on 'em."

"Damn them!" Barthen said furiously. "Damn them to hell! And you took it? You stood there and took it?"

"Yes, Ben. I stood there and took it."

"By God, *I* won't! I'll be in Holtville in the morning. Let the army keep me from goods I bought and paid for!"

"Wish you luck," Riker said drily, turning to Bogan. "Shake hands with the boss," he told him. "Ben, this is Bogan, out of Texas. I think he'll do."

"Glad to have you with us," Barthen said, touching hands briefly, measuring the tall man. "You handle a gun?"

"Some."

"And this is Conerley," Riker said. Beau put out his arm indifferently.

"You left-handed," Barthen asked, "or cross-draw?"

For answer, the Remington jumped into Beau's hand in a blur of effortless motion. Barthen smiled.

"What is your name?"

"I'm Beau Conerley."

"You're good, Conerley," Barthen told him. "And believe me, you're going to have to be."

"And this is Smith," Riker said then. The Englishman was standing stiffly erect. At the mention of his name he jerked his head slightly forward.

"Cyril Smith, sir. At your service."

"Smith," Riker said, "has some army background. Claims he worked with Ortega."

"Oh?" Barthen said, interested.

61

"I commanded the irregular regiment at San Jacinto," Smith said crisply. "Prior to that I served in the Royal Fusileers, during the uprising in India. My rank was major."

"Well, well, well," the owner commented. "And now you offer your services to Spread Eagle?"

"For reasons that are personal, sir," Smith said in his continuingly elegant fashion. "I would like to see this barbarian Ortega beaten ino the ground."

"So would I," Barthen said. "So would I."

"And I also think, Mr. Barthen, that I might be able to get that embargo lifted on your weapons shipment."

"How?"

The corners of the Englishman's mouth turned up in a sly smile. "There are ways," he said, "to beat the army at its own games. Not ethical, perhaps, but in war, as in love, all's fair."

"Come inside, Major," Barthen told him. "You look spent. A bath, a shave, a change of clothes—and then a long chat, eh?"

"Your grateful servant," Smith said.

"Come along then. Fran, show these boys their bunks and drop back here. Your journey to Holtville might have paid dividends." Barthen turned then, led the glib Cyril Smith inside the palatial *hacienda*.

"Y'see, Jess?" Beau said admiringly. "That Smitty's a gent who counts for somethin'. Jess?" Conerley raised his own eyes to where Bogan was looking, to a balcony on the third story of the house. A girl stood there, gazing down at Bogan, her figure revealed through the gauzelike nightgown she wore, her hair hanging long and touseled-looking, as if she had just come from bed.

"Well ain't that a sight," Beau Conerley said, his voice tight in his throat. "Jesus!"

"Forget it," Fran Riker told them. "The both of you."

"Belong to you?" Beau asked.

"She's family," Riker said. "The son's wife. Forget about her."

"I won't give her a second thought," Beau said, at the same time touching thumb and forefinger to the brim of his hat. From the balcony the girl returned the salute, made it seem very personal.

"Let's get some sleep," Bogan said. "Where's the bunkhouse?"

"I'll take you there," Riker said.

"Beau . . ."

"You boys go along. I'll catch up."

As he spoke, a man stepped onto the balcony—Carl Barthen, also in nightdress. He stared down at them, whirled to his wife and spoke sharply, unintelligibly to the three men below. But her laughter sounded clearly in the summer night's air—derisive, mocking, goading. He took her by the arm then, dragged her from the balcony.

"She don't look broken-in to me," Beau said thoughtfully. "Skittish as a filly in heat. . . ."

"I'll say it once more, gunfighter," Riker told him troubledly. "Put her out of your head. That was slick, that draw you showed the boss—but there's no defense at all against a bullet in the back."

"From you?"

"I'm foreman of Spread Eagle, Conerley. I'm ramrod. You cause grief at this ranch and you bought yourself an enemy. Hell, yes, I'd shoot you in the back."

"That's nice to know, cowman."

"I hope it gives you comfort, gunfighter."

"We're all of us getting a little edgy," Jess Bogan put in. "How about a night's good rest under our belts and start fresh in the morning?"

Riker reached up, gave Bogan an affectionate slap on the back.

"The ticket exactly," he said. "Let's go." The foreman started off, Bogan beside him. Conerley gave one more searching glance toward the balcony overhead and caught up with them.

"How long do you know Smith?" Riker asked Jess.

"Met him last night."

"Last night? I had an idea you knew him longer than that."

"Seems like that to me, too."

"Wish you'd told me, Jess," Riker said and Bogan laughed softly.

"Moves right in, don't he?" the big man commented.

"Yeh," Riker said, and then brightened. "But that's fine with me if he can deliver. God knows, this Mex is making us look bad. Making *me* look bad. If Smith can out-think Ortega, like he says, he's got me with him all the way." There was a pause. "How," Riker asked, "do you think he figures to get the embargo lifted on those guns?"

"He said it wouldn't be especially honest," Jess said. "But just what, I got no idea at all."

"Beat the army at their own game," Riker repeated. "How do you do that?"

"Don't worry about Smitty," Beau Conerley put in. "If he says he can do it, he'll do it."

From their left came the sound of riders, and a moment later two of them appeared, one leading a third horse with a body draped across the saddle. Bogan heard a soft groan escape from Riker's lips. The horsemen reined up.

"It's all over for Lew Cross," one said quietly. "He never even got his gun out."

Conerley walked to the dead man, looked at him with curiosity. "This is the same fella," he said. "I knew him over in—*Jesus!* Was he choked to death?"

"They ain't particular out there," the horseman growled bitterly.

"You were supposed to stay together," Riker said.

"Damnit, we were together! We were ridin' single file in that narrow spot through the cottonwoods—me, Whitey and Lew. We came out in the open and Whitey said, 'where's Cross?' So we went back. . . ." The rough voice trailed off.

"Helluva way for white men to fight," Beau said.

"You takin' a hand?"

"To sling lead, yeh," Beau answered uncertainly and drew a harsh laugh from the mounted man.

"That's what Lew thought," he said. "That's what we all thought. . . ."

"Who's still out there?" Riker broke in impatiently.

"Wightman, Rowe and Tanney. They counted eight more cows with their throats opened."

Riker sighed deeply. "All right, Al. Do the honors

64

for Lew, will you? I'll send Crown and McCrillus to finish your stint." He swung away toward the low-roofed adobe bunkhouse with Bogan and Conerley following.

"I'll go out," Jess volunteered but the foreman shook his head.

"I want you to see it by daylight first," he said. "There's a stream that winds all through the land, and thick groves to pick your way through."

"What do the Mex do, wait in the trees?"

"Sometimes with a knife lashed to a stick. Sometimes with a *garrotte*."

"Yellow bastards," Beau muttered.

"It's El Lupo's way," Riker told him. "Especially when he runs short of ammo."

"Who supplies him when he isn't short?"

"He used to sneak in here and steal ours till we stopped leaving it around handy. Now he raids the army patrols. His favorite time is just before dawn on Sunday, when practically the whole shebang is sleeping off their big Saturday drunk." Riker opened the screen door of the bunkhouse, lit a candle. There were eight cots on each side, less than half of them occupied, and at the far end of the narrow building a large table.

"These two be all right?" Riker asked.

"Fine with me," Jess said. He sat down gratefully, began pulling off his heavy work shoes and reminded himself to procure a pair of boots since the new job was in the saddle. Riker had moved further down and was waking two men.

"Let's go, Crown," he urged. "C'mon, McCrillus—up!" The one named McCrillus rolled out of his bunk quickly. The other man had an objection.

"Damnitall, Riker," he growled menacingly, "I just climbed into this sack. . . ."

"No help for it, Bill," the foreman told him. "Lew Cross is dead and we're short-handed out there."

Bill Crown raised himself to a sitting position. "They got Lew?"

Riker nodded grimly. "He let himself get separated," he said. "That's about all it takes."

65

"We'll see what they can take," Crown said and came to his feet. Bogan saw a curly-haired, darkly handsome man of his own age and inclinations. Jess liked the cut of him, liked the way he'd swallowed his gripe and jumped-to the moment the situation was explained to him. Crown was buckling his gunbelt when he took first notice of Bogan.

"A recruit," he said. "Two of 'em, by damn! Welcome to the lodge, boys—and don't think you won't earn your pay."

Riker introduced the four of them all around, his voice worried and impatient. Crown and McCrillus moved out into the night and Riker returned to the main house.

The cot didn't accommodate all of Bogan, but it was a rare bed that ever did and he settled himself as comfortable as he could.

"Jess?"

"Yeh, Beau."

"You think we made a smart move?"

"No."

"When you gonna talk with old Arnett?"

"Look him up in the morning. Probably bunks with the regular crew."

"Then let's take off."

"Afraid I got myself stuck here, kid."

"But, cristamighty, Jess—how you gonna fight some yellow dog that drops on you from a tree?"

"Damned if I know."

"Well, this son don't aim to find out. Not like Lew Cross found out."

"Don't blame you a bit," Jess told him.

"Hell, I'm a gunfighter."

"One of the best. 'Night, kid."

"Night." It was quiet for a full two minutes. Then, "Jess?"

"Yeh?"

"I think maybe I'll stick it for a week."

"Whatever you say, Beau. But I wouldn't stay on account of her."

"How'd you know what I was thinkin' about?"

"Just a guess. 'Night."

Beau let out a long breath. "All I got to do is close my

66

eyes," he said. "Man, she's so close I can reach out and touch her."

When Jess closed his eyes all he saw was trouble ahead.

THREE

Bogan opened his eyes and lay very still, not certain whether he had heard a sound outside or dreamed it. Through the window of the bunkhouse shone the dull gray light of pre-dawn, and that brought to mind something Riker had told him last night.

He swung his legs to the floor, stood up, and in the same flowing motion he was buckling the gun to his waist, then striding barefooted to the door. He pulled it open carefully, stepped outside.

Jess and the Mexican discovered each other in the same instant. The other man had his gun in his hand, brought it up with startled suddenness and fired. Bogan drove two shots into the very sound, saw the man spin and fall. A third gun opened up, kicking dust at his feet, sending a slug screaming past his eyes. He whirled, triggered twice and missed twice. Twice more he fired. The raider's body jerked, jerked again and collapsed in a heap. Then Bogan was running, racing to head off the third Mex before he regained his horse. The vaquero, slim and swift, vaulted into the saddle, wheeled the horse around. His intent was to ride Jess down, trample him, and out of pure desperation Bogan lunged for the animal's neck, held on perilously for a long moment and then kicked upward with his foot. The kick caught the man squarely in the chest, drove him high out of the saddle and off the horse completely. Jess dropped himself free with a jolt, rolled to his feet again and moved on the groggy-eyed, badly-shaken Mexican.

"*Tu te levanta!* On your feet!" he told him, and when the man didn't move Bogan reached down and hauled him erect.

"Some goin', Jessie," Beau Conerley called, coming up to him. There were figures hurrying toward them from all directions of the ranch. "Man, you had yourself a time!"

"Man," Jess mimicked drily, "I don't want another time like it."

"Fine, Bogan, fine!" Fran Riker told him happily. "Three of the bastards, by God!" He grabbed the man Jess was loosely holding, jerked him around. "And you and me, you dirty little killer, are going to have a talk, aren't we? All about El Lupo, hanh?"

"Me no sabe El Lupo," the Mexican said blandly. *"Me no sabe nada."*

"You'll know something when I'm through with you. Bring him along to the house, Bogan. Let's give the old man a look at him."

"Whatta you want done with these two?" a gunhand called to Riker. "One's dead and the other's dyin'."

"Take 'em out to where you found Lew Cross last night," Riker said stridently. "Let the sonofabitch bury his own dogs."

All that was happening now brought a frown to Bogan's rugged face. It was not that he couldn't appreciate either the foreman's elation or his bitterness, but so far as Jess was concerned the trouble with the Mexicans was still a very impersonal business. Riker had asked him for help and he was glad he could be of help, but he didn't want any part of this after-thing. The pair he had shot had been sent on a job—a damn risky job—and just because they had run out of luck was no reason, in Bogan's mind, to take away their dignity. When his own luck ran out, Bogan thought, he hoped the scudders would put him underground properly, not drag his carcass over the countryside like a side of beef.

And as for the one he'd taken alive, Bogan would just as soon now he'd gotten away. The vaquero had an Injun look about him—the high cheekbones, broad nostrils— and if he was he'd be proud, and stubborn, and unbreakable. Pit that against what Riker would want to know about El Lupo, what Riker might do to get that information, and Bogan got a picture that made his frown deepen.

"Bring him along, Jess," Riker said again.

"You're not going to get anything out of him."

"The hell I won't."

"Probably doesn't know anything, anyhow."

"What're you talking about? He knows where El Lupo is, doesn't he? He knows how many men he's got, what their supplies are? Come on, bring him along."

"If the Mex had you, Riker," Bogan persisted, "would you spill your guts about Spread Eagle?"

"They'd have to kill me," Riker said automatically, not even having to think about it. But then he did think about it and he scowled up at the tall man. "What was that supposed to mean, Jess?"

"That you're a proud son," Bogan told him. "Proud and loyal—but no more so than this fella. Ask me, and I say you'd save time and trouble by killing him right here and now. Just like they'd have to do to you."

Riker looked at Bogan for another long moment, then dropped his glance to the Mexican. Very slowly he drew the .45 from the holster on his hip, very deliberately pointed it between the dark-skinned vaquero's brown eyes.

"*Yo te mataré,*" Riker told the man with conviction enough to worry Bogan. "I am going to kill you."

The Mexican shrugged his slim shoulders, showed no other sign of emotion. Riker thumbed back the hammer. The metallic sound made the doomed man blink his eyes, just once. Bogan's hands were tightened into fists, every nerve in his body seemed to be jumping.

"*Vaya con Dios,*" Riker told him and the little vaquero only stood there, stone-faced, waiting for it. "Crista-mighty!" Riker said, letting the gun fall limply to his side. "I don't have sand in me to match that!"

And Bogan, out of his vast relief, his admiration, laughed aloud and whomped the bewildered Mexican a tooth-rattling thump on the back that all but drove him to his knees.

"*Valiente, amigo, valiente!*" Bogan assured him. "*Un hombre muy bravo—verdaderamente!*"

The Mexican recovered his balance, looked at both of them warily.

"What's this, Riker? What's going on here?" It was

69

Ben Barthen, with Smith a half-step behind—a shaved, trim-mustached, short-haired, important-looking Smith.

"Bogan made a catch, Ben. Our friend sent in a party of three to raid us in our own backyard. That's two of them we're sending back—and this scrawny little bugger here is a tougher nut than I want to crack."

The boss of Spread Eagle held out his hand to the towering Bogan, looked up into his face with an expression so baldly admiring as to be embarrassing.

"Bogan, you've earned yourself a bonus with this work," he said fervently. "By the Harry, you could be the man who can turn the tide for me . . ."

"Good work, Jess," Cyril Smith said, surprising Bogan twice: The use of his first name, the impunity with which he broke in on Barthen. That said, the Englishman swung to Riker. "What did you mean, Fran—a tougher nut than you'd want to crack?"

The foreman, too, seemed taken aback by the man's aggressiveness. And not a little miffed. When he answered it was to Barthen direct.

"This particular Mex isn't going to tell us a thing," he said. "In fact, it wouldn't surprise me one bit if he isn't pretty high up in El Lupo's army. . . ."

"The beggar's nothing but a breed," Smith broke in tartly. "With your permission, sir," he said in an entirely different tone to Barthen, "I'd like to question him."

"Go right ahead, Major."

Smith turned to the Mexican, spoke sneeringly, *"Ahora, campesino! Digame cuantos hombres con El Lupo?* How many men with El Lupo?"

"Me no sabe El Lupo."

Smith struck the man with the flat of his hand. The Mexican took it impassively, then sent a stream of dark betel juice at Smith's feet. Smith hit him again.

"Cuantos hombres?" he asked again.

"Mil diez," the Mex answered with a languid grin. There were ten thousand men. *"Viente, tal vez."* Maybe even twenty.

Smith swung his head to Barthen. "Dutch courage," he explained. "From that filthy betel nut he's chewing. I'd like another go at him in an hour or so. The sun will be hot then, and in India we made good use of the sun on types like this one."

"Whatever you say, Major. Meanwhile, let's go back to the house and breakfast. Then into Holtville to see about my shipment." Barthen swung around, retraced his steps to the *hacienda* with 'The Major' on his flank.

"I'll be damned," Fran Riker said softly. "Bogan, you figure maybe I lost my job?"

"I hope not, mister," Jess told him. "Smith ain't the man I'd want running this show."

"Smitty sure changed some," Beau put in. "Hell, he looked right through me—and I saved his life for him."

There was a welcome sound then, the cook calling them for morning chow. Riker looked at Bogan.

"Take the Mex over to that little storeroom," he said, "and lock him inside. Then come eat at my table."

Bogan led the vaquero toward the windowless hut Riker had indicated.

"Como se llama, hombre?" he asked him conversationally.

"Miguel."

"You fought in the war with Ortega?"

"Maybe."

"Then you know *el Ingles?*"

Miguel spat contemptuously. *"Que cobarde!"* he said.

"Why do you call him a coward?"

"El tenio miedo. He was afraid. He gave up without a fight."

"This was the affair at San Jacinto?" Bogan asked.

"San Jacinto, *si.* It brought great shame to our General."

They had reached the hut and now Bogan held the door open to the dark, steamy little room. Miguel stepped inside.

"El Ingles is going to make it hard for you," Bogan told him. "If the things he asks are of no importance, why not tell him?"

"Nada," the man said. "I tell nothing."

"Pues mente uno poco," Bogan suggested. "Then lie just a little bit. Not a big one like the ten thousand men."

"What is it to you, *hombre?"*

Bogan looked down into that rock-hard face. *"Nada,"*

71

he said unhappily. "Nothing, I guess." He closed the door, bolted it and started back, his mind full of Miguel of Mexico and Smith of England. It could just be that Bogan of West Texas had gotten himself on the wrong side of the fence in this argument.

"Psst!"

The sound brought his head around sharply.

"Over here, brother. Over here."

It was Branch Arnett, standing conspiratorially by a corner of the ranch hands' bunkhouse, his white-whiskered face and dancing blue eyes as familiar as ever. Bogan grinned as he walked to him.

"By Judas, I thought that was you with the big boss. Highest pockets I ever seed. What in tarnation you doin' with the gun crew, boy? How come you—"

"Soft, old man. Slow down. How are you, anyhow?"

"Sonny," Arnett said, "you remember how bad off I used to be in Paso? Well now I'm worse off."

"I met your granddaughter," Bogan said. "Why didn't you stay there and fix that spread up?"

"Don't tell me my business, dangit! Sure—fix it up. Work night and day, get the place spankin' fine. And then that play actin' son-in-law decides to come back and take over. Sure."

More than likely, Bogan thought, looking around. They seemed to be alone and he reached beneath his shirt for the leather pouch he had been carrying all these weeks.

"What you got there, boy?"

"You tell me," Bogan said, loosening the thongs. "Cup your hand here." Arnett did and Bogan poured out some of the sand-colored stuff. The old man was open-mouthed, his eyes staring at what he held in his palm. He reached with his free hand, pinched off a few grains and raised them to his lips. His tongue came out and he laid the stuff there, tasting it and sniffing alternately.

"Well?"

"It's mineral," Arnett said sagely.

"Oh, hell," Bogan said. "Sure it's mineral. But what mineral?"

"Can't tell. You take it out of the mountain?"

Bogan nodded.

"What you doin' way up here then? Why ain't you makin' yourself a couple, three million dollars?"

"Came up for an assay. Then, old man, we got to make a deal."

"Me? You mean me?"

"Yeh. But where can I get an assay done?"

"Government office's up to Westmorland. Only one you can trust in this thievin' country. Sonny, you mean you tracked all the way here to cut me out a share?"

Bogan nodded and the old man burst out laughing.

"And I'm the one that's supposed to be half looney," he said. "You're the crazy one, you and the other. . . . Say, did you end up pluggin' that sidekick you had?"

"No," Bogan told him, laughing himself. "Conerley's here with me."

"I figured you'd have to take strong measures with that proddy rannihan. Surprised you didn't."

"Yeh. What kind of work you doing here?"

"Oh, kinda assistant this and assistant that. This spread's at war, boy. You don't ranch and fight both."

"How about journeying up to Westmorland, then—getting the assay?"

"Alone?"

"Why not?"

"You'd trust me? To take this dust up there, and then come back and tell you what the office said?"

"Seems like you've done all the trusting up till now," Bogan said. "When do you think you can leave?"

"I'll ask the straw boss for the day off."

"Good." Bogan handed him the entire pouch, some five hundred dollars worth if it was the real McCoy.

Arnett took it, dropped it inside his old work shirt.

"See you when you get back," Bogan told him. "Take care of yourself." Arnett had a curious expression, almost sad. "What's the matter?"

"You know somethin'? I clean forget your name."

Bogan patted him gently on the shoulder. "Bogan," he told him. "Jess Bogan." Then he went to eat.

2

The wonder of it was, when Ben Barthen and 'Major' Smith returned from Holtville they had two wagonloads of new guns and cartridges with them. Fran Riker rode out to meet the small cavalcade with mixed emotions.

"It worked!" the boss of Spread Eagle said triumphantly. "The Major tricked those army boys right out of their boots!"

"How?" the foreman asked glumly.

"Oh, a little sleight of hand, you might say. How's that, Major—a little sleight of hand?"

"Capital, sir. Very good."

Riker just sat astride his horse, unsmiling, awaiting an answer to his question.

"The Major ran across a patrol yesterday," Barthen explained, his voice still jovial. "He was helping Bogan and the other fellow find their way into the Territory—which reminds me. Just what do we know about this Bogan jasper?"

Riker looked briefly at Smith, then to the owner.

"Not much, Ben," he said. "Except that he's some handy to have on the payroll. As you thought, yourself, around dawn this same day."

"I mean his background. How does he come to be in Mexico in the midst of hostilities?"

"He didn't say," Riker answered levelly, "and I didn't ask him." His head swung to Smith, smiling involuntarily. "You helped Bogan, did you, General?"

"Just Major, Fran," Smith replied with his own cold smile. "It happens we're fighting a general, though. And these weapons might be of some help."

"Yes, yes," Barthen said. "I was telling you how the Major foxed those soldier boys. He had a letter, you see, from the Lieutenant commanding this patrol company. Very nice letter, as a matter of fact, to the Colonel commanding the district. Well, b'God, what do you think he did last night? He wrote a very official note of his own, absolutely perfect, and he copied that Lieutenant's hand so even he couldn't swear he didn't pen it himself. Big flourishing signature and all, ordering that stupid depot sergeant to release the shipment to me." Barthen laughed heartily. "Wonderful, wonderful," he said. "Never enjoyed anything more."

"But just a ruse, sir," Smith said deprecatingly. "What's important now is to put these arms to work against the enemy. I suggest I begin my serious questioning of our prisoner."

"Right," Barthen said. "That's the positive attitude I've been looking for."

"What you've been getting, Ben," Riker asked, "that's been lacking?"

"Fran, we've been going at this all wrong. This is no cattle fight, some action against common rustlers. We're at war, man. For our very lives. What we've been 'lacking,' as you put it, is a military mind, a soldier's way of thinking these things out."

"Am I getting my walking papers?"

"Most certainly not!" Ben Barthen didn't say that, Cyril Smith did. Riker looked at him in amazement.

"Most certainly not," Smith said again. "Fran, if any man is absolutely vital to this cause, barring Mr. Barthen himself, then it is you. But this *is* war, and I'm a soldier. War is my profession. Soon there will be peace at Spread Eagle. El Lupo will be brought to bay. You will have no more use for a soldier and I'll go on my way . . ."

"There'll always be a place at Spread Eagle for you, Major," Barthen interjected.

"No, no. Let's not put sentiment before reality. Fran, I have only one mission, one simple ambition—to destroy this Mexican devil. You and I will shake hands across his grave, and I'll ride away."

"But until then," Riker said, "you're the new major-domo?"

Smith said nothing, turned his head to Barthen eloquently.

"You run my ranch, Fran," the owner said. "The Major will run my war."

Riker lowered his eyes, stared at the work-hardened hands gripping the reins. Then his head came up.

"So be it, Ben," he said. "Good luck, Major."

75

3

All in all, Ben Barthen thought when he was back in the spacious *hacienda* again, all in all his affairs looked to be on the upturn. He was especially pleased with himself, with the good judgment he had shown last night about Major Smith.

Smith had told him quite a story about himself—how the British army had sent him to act as a neutral observer of the war, how the damnable Mexicans had pressed him into service because of his tactical skill, and then thrown him into prison because his sympathies were with the American side. But he'd escaped, and in the course of it helped Bogan and Conerley to freedom. Quite a story.

Barthen congratulated himself on recognizing a diamond in the rough, on spotting the man's keen military mind and old world manners. He also liked the Englishman's deference to him, and as he sat in his study drinking coffee the owner of Spread Eagle found himself resenting the easy familiarity of Riker. As Smith said, that bred contempt. His foreman, Barthen decided, shouldn't call him 'Ben'. . . .

"Morning, Father," his son Carl said from the doorway.

"Morning, you say? Is it still morning?" Some of his impatience was with his son's garb. He looked like a New York clerk.

"It's not quite ten yet," Carl Barthen told him. He was a slender and pale-looking young man, with little physical resemblance to his father and none of Ben's vigor.

"You'll find that the day begins at the first crack of dawn on this ranch," the elder Barthen said. "Is your wife up yet?"

"Miriam's dressing. Speaking of dawn, she told me there was quite a commotion out by the men's quarters around that time. Said some men were shot."

"Good Lord, get that frightened look out of your face. There was a shooting out there and two men were killed. They happened to be Mexican raiders, and in case it has slipped your mind, Spread Eagle happens to be at war."

"Father," Carl said, "I really am trying to get used to your way of living—to the way everyone lives out here. It's

76

very hard to accustom myself to this business of men taking the law into their own hands. . . ."

"You mean men fighting their own battles?"

"Yes, I guess I mean that, too. But in the East a man can fight his own battles, as you say, without resorting to violence. It's more a contest of minds . . ."

His father's harsh laughter cut him short. "A contest of minds, eh? And out in this country any simple fool can do what I've done—is that your idea?"

"No, Father. Not at all. Of course it takes brains, and skill, and—well, I guess *shrewdness*—"

"You're damn well told it takes shrewdness. And you don't learn ranching by staying in bed half the day."

Carl looked uncomfortable. "Father," he said, "I'm afraid I made a wrong assumption."

"What assumption was that?"

"When you wrote that you'd like to see me again, to meet my wife—I guess I assumed it was going to be in the nature of a vacation. I didn't realize you wanted me to learn ranching."

"You're my son, aren't you?"

"Yes, I'm your son. But I didn't know you felt much about our relationship."

"Those are ideas your mother planted in your head. I've always wanted you to come out here and take over. But now I don't know. I don't think *you* want to make your life out here."

"But I do!" Carl insisted. "I do very much."

"Have you talked about it with your wife?"

"No, I haven't. This may sound a little strange, but Miriam and I don't seem to talk about serious matters at all."

"It's high time you did talk about serious matters," Barthen said. "And it's past time that you took that little lady down a few notches."

"What do you mean?"

"I mean, damnit, tighten your reins on her! Tell her to dress like a respectable married woman, not some dance-hall floozie. Tell her to stop parading herself around the men's quarters . . ."

"Am I really so much trouble, Father-in-law?" the girl

77

herself asked, coming into the room. "Do I look like a floozie this morning?"

"I'm not sorry you overheard me, young lady," Barthen told her. "And if my opinion means anything, then I'll say that your dress is not modest. Why, you're half coming out of it! And your ankles are exposed for every Tom, Dick and Harry to see!"

"Are they so ugly?" she asked coquettishly, inching the skirt even higher. Miriam was a blonde-haired, green-eyed girl with a round, voluptuous figure, a round, pretty face and a provocative mouth.

"Do you permit your wife to behave like this?" Barthen demanded of his son.

"Maybe you'd better change into something else," Carl said timidly. "I guess you do dress sort of—different for a ranch."

"But all my clothes are like this, Carl, and you know it. You said you liked me to be in the latest fashion."

"But they have different ideas of fashion out here," he said, growing more ill-at-ease by the second.

"All right!" she said angrily. "I'll just lock myself in my room all day. Maybe then I won't offend anyone's morals!"

"Now, Miriam," Carl said, but the girl had already turned, with a whirl of the skirt that revealed very attractive legs, and strode from the room stormily.

"Let her go," Ben Barthen said to his son. "Let her stay in her room until she's ready to dress as she should."

"But you don't know her when she's like this, Father. She's got a terrible temper."

"Then take a strap to her, damnit! A good tanning will show her who's wearing the pants!"

"Beat her?" Carl asked incredulously. "Do men beat women out here?"

"They whip the ones that need whipping, by God! And if I ever saw a dossie that needed one it's your wife."

Carl shook his head. "I couldn't," he said. "I couldn't do that."

"Then you're nò man for this country," his father growled, getting to his feet, picking up his hat from the desk and setting it on his head furiously. "And unless you change your ways damn soon," Barthen added, "you're no man for me." With that he, too, went out, leaving his son with a dilemma that wasn't going to be easily solved.

4

"How the hell big is this range, anyhow?" Beau Conerley asked in a complaining voice. They had been in the saddle since seven, now it was the hot blaze of noon, and the third gunhand riding with them kept insisting that they had not yet reached the limit of their particular patrol.

"Barthen takes big bites," Bogan agreed.

"And swallows it whole," the man named Crown said. "Least he did over in Arizona Territory."

"How does he know this is California U.S.?" Jess asked him. Crown, square-jawed and intent smiled lazily at the question.

"He says it's U.S.," the rider said. "That makes it so."

"Except to El Lupo."

"Yeh. The trouble with that Mex is he used to own some of this graze personal. Built the *hacienda* himself, so I'm told."

Bogan hadn't known this, hadn't been told about it by Riker, and now he considered the thing thoughtfully. Beau Conerley put his own feelings into words.

"Can't blame the Mex for pressin' so hard," he said.

"Guess not," Crown said. "But hell, who's ever right or wrong in a fight like this?"

"The man that pays me," Beau said. "He's always right."

Crown laughed. "You got the spirit, kid. Hey, looka yonder!"

Yonder, by some half mile, rode another group of horsemen. Six, Jess guessed, and identifiable by their sombreros as Mexican.

"What's the program, Crown?" Jess asked the older hand.

"My instructions are cut and dried. Kill every Mex you find." So saying, he slipped the rifle from its boot, put his horse at a sharp canter. After a hundred yards he fired his first shot. Jess and Beau followed suit, kept closing the

79

distance, kept peppering the other party with rifle fire. They, in their own turn, seemed to be at odds with themselves. Two riders broke obliquely from the pack to meet the attack head-on. The other four pulled up short, began waving their arms excitedly, and when the first pair found themselves alone they also reined in, got off a brief salvo and wheeled around again.

Bogan found himself grinning in relief, found himself holding back the stallion so eager to overtake the retreating horses. He had fired the carbine four times, each bullet high and wide, and now he realized that Beau's definition of right and wrong no longer held for him. Spread Eagle was the transgressor here, and Bogan could take no pride in whatever help he rendered.

Crown held up his hand and they halted the pursuit.

"Ten more minutes of this and we'll be right where they want us," he said sagely. "It's my private guess that Lupo headquarters in the canyon beyond that thick pine grove."

"How many ride for him?"

"Some week they're thick as locusts. Next week you don't spot a damn one." Crown spat, looked at Bogan steadily. "This week he's been powerful busy," he said. "Includin' that scout party this mornin'. Anybody asked me, I'd say he's ready for the big push against Spread Eagle."

"So long as he does the pushin' that's fine with me," Beau said. "So long as he sticks to gunplay."

"Don't count on it, kid," Crown told him. "Don't count on anything."

The three of them doubled back then, rode for another long hour in the broiling sun before they reached the chuck wagon. In the midst of chow a rider came out from the *hacienda*. Everybody was wanted back there, pronto.

FOUR

Smith had broken Miguel. It had taken two hundred and fifty-six minutes in a temperature of one hundred and twenty-five degrees, but in the end he had cracked the little Mexican's very mind, plucked the information he wanted from it and then threw the raving, agonized vaquero back into the black and airless storeroom.

The torture Smith used was crude and simple, and despite his claims that the British army had originated it in India, most of those who witnessed it at Spread Eagle knew that it was a favorite with the Apaches, who had learned it at the hands of the Spaniards, who had been using it since the time of the Inquisition three hundred years before. Miguel had merely been stripped naked, then spread out on a rock slab in the open sun, like a five-pointed star. Each wrist and ankle was fastened taut to a leather thong, the end of each thong lashed to a wooden stake hammered into the ground. All that remained then was to douse the leather bindings with heavily salted water and wait for the merciless sun to shrink the thongs, make them contract at a rate that was imperceptible to the human eye—but an ecstasy of pain to the victim. A very special pain, a kind that began very slowly, almost pleasantly, that increased very slowly, degree by degree, minute by minute, got to a rather exquisite point where a man could measure his misery in seconds, tick them off in his head with the certainty that it was going to be worse and worse and worse.

When the Apaches stretched an enemy's tendons he generally sat around and watched the process, as his Spanish teacher had done. Smith's little touch was to leave Miguel completely alone for thirty-minute periods, then revive his flagging consciousness with a bucket of salted water thrown full in his face.

81

"How many men with El Lupo?"
"No sabe."
"Where do they camp?"
"No sabe."
"I'll be back in thirty minutes."

Smith made the trip eight times, asked the identical two questions. Seven times he got varying answers, from *"no sabe"* to "ten thousand" to hysterical laughter. The eighth time Miguel was so insane with his anguish that his voice was calm and toneless, as if temporarily disembodied from the hell he was experiencing. He spoke, in fact, at the mere sound of Smith's own horribly familiar voice, without even making sense any more of the question.

"Tenemos cinquenta hombres," he said. *"Estamos en El Canon de los Dos Bocas."* Fifty of them, in the canyon with both ends open.

Smith, suspecting this was the truth, called the prostrate man a liar, said he would be back in thirty minutes.

"Cinquenta hombres el canon dos bocas," Miguel repeated, running his words together dully. Then a piercing scream was wrenched from his throat and after that there was nothing intelligible to be gotten out of him.

"Well, what do we do about it?" Ben Barthen asked his military adviser back at the house.

"Attack," Smith said without hesitation. "Bottle him up in that canyon and finish him off."

"With what?" Fran Riker said. "I've got ten against his fifty."

"We," Smith said pointedly, "have surprise. Ten gun-fighters, I grant you, but tonight we will look like three hundred."

"You can't go after El Lupo at night," Riker said. "Even if you had the three hundred. . . ."

"In India," Smith said urbanely, "I was given precisely the same advice by a subaltern who supposedly knew what he was talking about. One must never attack the natives on their home territory after dark. The fallacy of that, friend Riker, is that the native begins to feel himself immune as soon as the sun goes down. Well, I did attack the beggars that night. It was, if I may say so, a complete rout. We caught the enemy in his tents."

"You won't catch El Lupo sleeping," Riker said stubbornly. "He'll cut us to ribbons out at that canyon."

Smith spread his arms, looked to the attentive Barthen.

"There seems to be a difference of opinion," he said. "The layman chooses to disagree with the professional. Sir, the decision is yours."

Barthen pulled at his lower lip. "What Riker says—well, there's a lot to side him. These Mex send out little parties during the day, just to spy on us. But they mostly siesta when the sun's up, do their work at night. They'll be ready for us if we come at them tonight."

"I bow to your judgment, sir," Smith said immediately. "Now I suggest we attack within the hour."

"Impossible," Riker said. "I got six fighters out on the range."

"Recall them," Smith said, and it was a direct order. "They're hardly any good out there if Ortega is snug in his canyon."

The foreman looked to his boss, his face plainly showing his disagreement. But Barthen shook him off.

"Bring everybody in," he said. "Let's see how we stack up and then make our plans."

That was when the rider was sent out to the chuck wagon. Crown, Bogan and Conerley returned first, then Wightman, Rowe and Tanney. Rogero, Heilman and a youngster named McCrillus completed the roster of Spread Eagle's warriors who all assembled in the courtyard for a council. Ben Barthen stood on the steps of the *hacienda* and addressed them.

"You're a fine looking crew and I'm proud of you," the owner began. "No man could ask for better. But as all of you must know this war has taken a terrible toll." He raised his arm and pointed to a field beyond the bunkhouses. "There's twenty-eight good friends lying out there. They paid the most, and there's no denying it. My own personal losses don't stack up to theirs, but I will tell you this: The drain on Spread Eagle has reached the point where I might have to toss in the sponge. And, boys, that means those twenty-eight loyal sons have laid down their lives for nothing. . . ."

Jess Bogan was watching the man and listening to him with interest. Obviously, Barthen was going to ask this crew he was so proud of to do something real special. And the crew would do it all right, whatever it was, though they were probably going to feel that they'd all but volunteered. Then it came:

"We found out that Ortega's got fifty men," Barthen said, "and we also found out that he operates out of that double pass canyon. Now it's always been my contention that the five best Mexicans that ever drew breath add up to one medium good Yank. It's also my contention that the Mex can't fight worth a damn when the sun is out. So I'm proposing, here and now, that we break this war open. What do you say?"

Someone, of course, should have shouted "Let's get 'em!", and if Fran Riker had asked them to attack someone would have. But the foreman was standing off to one side, arms folded across his chest, clearly disassociating himself from the plan.

"Let's hear from the ramrod," the fighter named Rowe suggested. "Speak up, Fran."

Riker raised his head, looked from Barthen to the crew.

"No man here wants to win this fight more than I do," he said emotionally. "No man wants it over quicker than I do. But attacking Lupo where he lives is just about what I'd want if I were Lupo. When the odds are against you, I say that's when you play it close. You keep whittling away till you got a gambling chance. . . ."

"That's negative thinking," Cyril Smith broke in, earning himself a general look of displeasure from the crew. "Mr. Barthen has told us that his resources are nearly gone. He can't afford to play your waiting game. . . ."

"Mister," Riker shot back, "I know Spread Eagle's affairs as well as Ben, himself, does. I know we got to make a move soon. My idea is to ride out to that bivouac you and Bogan ran across. We'll tell the army what we're up against here and ask for help."

The crew approved that if Smith did not. Barthen saw that they did and held up his hand for attention.

GUNS OF REVENGE

"That sounds good to me," he said. "I'll head up the delegation myself, Riker, and you and Major Smith come along. We'll start at once."

Riker added the ones he thought would make the best impression for Spread Eagle, left five men behind to guard against any raid. Bogan went with him, Conerley stayed at the ranch, an arrangement that suited Beau fine.

For when Barthen first began his little speech, Conerley's roving glance had been directed to the balcony overhead, to the face and bare shoulders of the blonde girl peering down at the men in the courtyard. Her glance, too, was roving—and when it met with Beau's she smiled at him. The redhead heard practically nothing of the debate that followed, so intent was he on the progress of the flirtation. Several times Bogan nudged him with a rough elbow, and each time he told the big man to let him be. Then the meeting broke up, the blonde head disappeared from view, and when Bogan rode off with his party Conerley walked back to the bunkhouse deep in his personal thoughts.

Miriam had noted from her window who it was who left the camp and who stayed, and her eyes lingered appraisingly on the broad shoulders and slim waist of the young cowboy whose brazen, devil-may-care smile had been a match for her own moments ago. There was something wild about him, something that reached out and kindled the fire of her own recklessness even higher. And he reminded her of someone she had known back in Hartford, her home town. A man named Phil Shaw, a married man from Boston who traveled for a ladies' wear concern throughout New England. Miriam had been sixteen when she first met him, a chance encounter in Meyer's Department Store, and without any of the formalities that other young men went through, the salesman had promptly invited her for a buggy ride that night.

She'd accepted, but when she learned that he was married she demanded that he turn the buggy around and take her back to her aunt's house. Shaw had laughed, told her to suit herself and brought her home. She remembered that laugh, as if she had behaved childishly, and remembered his face, his clothes, his worldly air. And when he

85

passed through Hartford a month later she 'happened' to run into him outside his hotel. He asked her again to go riding with him, and they came back long after midnight. A week later she was with him again, in a cheap hotel in Bridgeport, and the affair continued for nearly six months. His company changed his itinerary then, sent him down into the New York territory, and Miriam took several train rides to Manhattan to continue their trysts. But one night they had a quarrel, something trivial, and broke off. Miriam never saw Phil Shaw again, but the red-haired cowboy reminded her of him.

She wore now a thin, open necked wrapper, and on the rug at her feet was the dress she had ripped off and torn in her first ungovernable burst of temper. But though anger still burned in her she realized that destroying the dress wouldn't show her husband and his father anything at all. That was what they wanted, actually, and she could hear Ben Barthen's voice again, telling Carl to tighten the reins on her—'*stop parading around the men's quarters. . . .*'

Miriam looked in the mirror, found herself smiling wickedly at the reflection. She let the wrapper fall from her shoulders, crossed to the large closet. From it she took down a bright red skirt, one with a hemline even shorter than the new Eastern fashion decreed. She fastened the skirt to her waist and chose a thin white cotton blouse, pulled it over her blonde head and moved the shoulders down even with her forearms. The effect of the costume in the mirror shocked even the reckless Miriam. But then her resentment flared anew, put any qualms about the consequences out of her mind. As a final touch she unpinned her hair, let it hang low over her bare back in thick, golden blonde waves, then left the room and made her way out of the house via the servants' wing.

She was a sultry match for that bright sunny afternoon as she strolled with feigned casualness in the direction of the bunkhouses. Along her route was the corral, and Miriam tarried there to ask light and foolish questions about the horses. The answers she got were curtly given, almost surly, for a female was the one commodity the ranch hands didn't want bedeviling their thoughts now.

One, an old-timer named Stoney who had been at Spread Eagle so long he remembered Ben Barthen's wife, felt compelled to give the boss' daughter-in-law a few words of advice.

"I'd stick close to the mainhouse, missy," he told her.

"But there's nobody there to talk to," she answered innocently.

"There's your husband."

She shook her head. "He's not even there to keep me company," she said with a childish pout. "He went off riding by himself."

"Well, I wouldn't go no further than this corral gate," Stoney cautioned impatiently. "We're ordinary cowmen here and know our place. But them . . ." He moved his head from side to side.

"Why are they different?"

"Cause they're nothin' but gunslicks, that's why. Just a bunch of drifters who turn up where the trouble is."

"And they don't know their place?" Miriam said blandly, slanting her eyes at the old man.

"They'd insult you, missy. And more, if they thought they could get away with it. You heed me now. Go on back to the house."

"I think you're just trying to frighten me," she said. "But I'm going to take your dare—"

"I wasn't darin' you!" Stoney protested. "I was warnin' you!"

She moved away from him with a swing of her supple hips, came closer to the forbidden bunkhouse with the excitement heightening in her breast. After a month here Miriam knew how lonely all these men were, but not until now had she realized they were divided into two classes, that the one who had flirted with her belonged to a special, and dangerous, breed.

All at once there was a figure standing in the doorway of the low slung building, hands on his hips, flat-crowned hat pushed back to reveal close-cropped red hair, smiling at her impudently and looking for all the world as if she'd been expected at this place at this particular time.

Beau stepped from the doorway, walked toward the

blonde girl with the same rolling, confident gait she affected. The difference was, and Miriam knew it, he *was* sure of himself.

"I was just comin' after you," Beau said.

"Coming—after me?"

"Up to the house. Be a lot more comfortable."

"You know who I am, don't you?" She was all off balance. "I'm married. My husband's father—"

"I know," Beau said. "And I know where your husband is right now, he's reading a book down by the river. And the old man is off on a trip. That leaves the house empty, except for a cook who's takin' siesta."

The girl was assailed by the animal vitality of him—the violence—and she saw how vividly he and his kind stood apart from every other man she had ever encountered. And all the time that she was being so afraid she had never felt such a compelling attraction.

"Who's your friend, kid?" asked a heavy voice and Miriam's startled eyes went beyond Conerley to a dark-visaged man in the same doorway.

"*My* friend, that's who," Conerley said belligerently. "Get back in your cage."

Then another face was there, just as ominous. Especially when he grinned at her.

"Come on in, baby," he invited. "You're just what this place needs. . . ."

The red-headed one closed his strong, freckled hand on her arm, turned her around and began leading her away.

"What are you doing? Let me go!"

"It's too damn crowded around here," Beau said. "Let's go to the barn."

"No! I'm not going anywhere with you. . . ."

"Then why'd you get all tricked-out like that for me?"

"I didn't!"

"And you didn't give me the eye from your room a while ago?"

"That didn't mean anything! I can smile at somebody, can't I?"

"Not like that you can't. Not at me."

"And who do you think you are?"

88

"Honey, I'm Beau Conerley," he explained. "The gun-fighter."

They were at the barn. Beau pulled the door open, brought her inside the high-ceilinged, half-darkened place.

"Say, this is all right," he said. "This is fine." He led her to the ladder that rose to the hayloft. "Go on up."

"I won't," Miriam said. "You're not nice at all."

Beau slipped his arm around her waist, pulled her close and kissed her the only way he knew how. She pushed at him, resisted, then suddenly went limp, sagged against his hard chest with a moan.

"Go on," Beau said. "Climb."

She looked at his mouth, smoky-eyed, and smiled. Then she turned and climbed the ladder.

Carl Barthen had decided to take his problem away from the house, beyond the conflicting influences of his headstrong young wife and strong-willed old father. The truth was that he knew neither of them very well at all, yet each one had assumed a vital importance in his life—and each was pulling him in an opposite direction.

Nor was the young man even sure of his emotions to-ward them. On the first morning of their marriage Carl had looked at the girl in the bed beside him and asked himself if this was really the person he was going to love and cherish for the rest of his life, or had he only married to possess her, to lock up the excitement she could bring a man. After six months he still wondered.

As to his father, Carl was intelligent enough to under-stand that he had been reunited with Ben Barthen carry-ing in his mind some pre-conceived opinions of nearly twenty years standing. That was his mother's legacy—a picture of a cold, ruthless man whose total existence was devoted to the acquisition of wealth and power. And not an entirely distorted picture, Carl thought, although there was no mistaking his father's human qualities—the desire for a son who would follow in his own footsteps; the con-viction that the West was pure and heroic, the East a new Sodom; the objection to Miriam's clothes. But it seemed to the son that his father did lay too much importance on

89

land and cattle, that he saw himself as the founder of some dynasty of ranchers who would rule an empire bigger than the late Bonaparte's.

And at that point the person of Carl Barthen emerged in Carl Barthen's own thoughts. What sort of person he was he had no idea. What he *wasn't,* he was positive, was a rancher.

Even the basic fundamentals of the business staggered his imagination. The day after his arrival he had been put on a huge, mean, unruly horse, nearly thrown over its head, and taken by his father on a seemingly endless journey to the grazeland. There, in a great, bawling, disorganized mass were the cattle. His father had explained that men took horses into that tangle, drove the beasts to round-up, put them on trails to market that extended for a thousand miles through the ruggedest of country. He had explained it with the implication that that was what Carl would have to do as the heir to Spread Eagle.

And as if the rudiments of ranching weren't enough, here he was with a range war to witness. The ordinary cowboys looked hardened enough, but they were harmless as draymen compared to the ones who rode in and out of the place with guns at their hip, rifles jutting from their saddles. And hardly a day passed that one wasn't brought in dead, that there wasn't a new grave dug in the field beyond the bunkhouses.

The flare-up at the house this morning had forced Carl into a decision. On the surface he had to choose between a life on Miriam's terms—going back East to a prosaic career in New York, Boston, Philadelphia—or a life out here under the domination of his father. He had come to the riverside to think it out, to weigh the considerations on either side. Now, at about the time that his father was riding to the army bivouac for help, that his wife was climbing into the hayloft with a gunman, Carl's decision was made. He closed the *Life of Plato* that he had been idly perusing, got to his feet and walked back to the ranch.

Old Stoney intercepted him as he was crossing the courtyard, thinking of the words he would say to his father, the instructions to Miriam to prepare for their leaving.

"Are you your father's son?" the cowman demanded.

"Yes," Carl said. "Whatever that means."

"He's got her in the barn."

"What?"

"The gunslick that joined up last night. With your missus." Stoney waited. "Well? What you goin' to do about it?"

Carl looked at the screwed-up, outraged face, his own mind stupified.

"I don't know," he said.

"Here," Stoney said, shoving an old singleshot into his hand. "Don't miss with this. You only get one chance."

Carl looked down at the enormous, unwieldy-looking gun, nodded his head dumbly. Then he began walking toward the barn, in a trance, like a man walking in his sleep. He reached the building, opened the door.

"Miriam?" he called, stepping inside. "Miriam?"

A voice answered from above.

"Go back outside," Beau Conerley told him, his voice strangely subdued. "Go back to the house."

"Is my wife up there?"

"Just go back to the house, mister."

Carl crossed to the ladder, still like a sleepwalker, began mounting the rungs.

"Go back," Beau said. Barthen looked up at him, saw a man his own age, kept climbing the ladder. Now he was at the top, gazing into the loft itself. Huddled in a corner was Miriam, holding the cotton blouse in front of her naked body. The red skirt and underclothes lay scattered beside a makeshift bed of hay.

"He made me, Carl!" she suddenly screamed. "He made me come here! I was just out for a walk—he forced me in here!"

Beau looked over his shoulder at her, a curious smile on his face, then turned back to the man on the ladder. And, for himself at least, just in time. Carl had the old gun upraised, aimed point-blank. Conerley's boot lashed out a split second before the .44 roared deafeningly in his ears. The long barrel was deflected upwards and the bullet imbedded itself into the ceiling overhead. Beau acted then on pure reflex, without seeing that it was a single-action weapon. He drove his fist down into the other man's face.

91

Carl's hands lost their grip on the ladder and he fell twelve feet through the air to the floor below, lay there unconscious.

Miriam darted from her corner, knelt over the edge of the loft and stared down at the figure of her husband.

"Now you've done it!" she said shrilly. "You've killed him!"

"I doubt it," Beau said with the same new calmness in him. "What was the idea of tellin' him you were raped?"

"I don't know, Beau. I just—it was the awful way he was looking at me. . . ."

"A few minutes ago you were sayin' how much you loved me," Beau reminded her. "How I was the only man you ever wanted again."

"I do, I do! Oh, Beau, I do love you!"

Carl Barthen heard his wife clearly. *Apparently,* he thought, *I made the wrong decision . . .*

2

One look at the old man's stormy face as he emerged from the HQ tent told Bogan that the mission had been in vain. And a brief nod from Fran Riker, walking at Barthen's shoulder, was a signal to mount up and return to Spread Eagle as empty-handed as they'd arrived.

"Ride out!" Barthen commanded unnecessarily, swinging into the saddle and jerking his horse around. "The great fighting army of the United States!" he shouted contemptuously. "The fire-eating conquerors of California! Get me away from the yellow stench of them!"

With that he raked spurs along the horse's ribs, set his back squarely to the figure of the Lieutenant who had appeared in the tent's opening. Cyril Smith kicked his own mount to a quick run, posted himself just off Barthen's right flank. The other Spread Eagle riders saw no need to hurry and followed more leisurely.

"Christmas in San Antone, Bogan!" a tremendous voice bellowed. "A return match!" Bogan grinned, waved back at the hulking figure of Sergeant Bronco, with whom he had been reunioning during Barthen's unsuccessful parley.

As so often happens, the brawl between the two giants had made them friends to the end.

"What's he talking about?" Riker asked.

"Just joking," Jess said. "He's going to quit the army and the two of us are going to get rich giving prizefights. What happened at your meeting?"

"We got some very bad news," Riker said worriedly. "The Lieutenant got orders just this morning to break camp and pull back to El Centro. Apparently the border has finally been set in Washington."

"At El Centro?"

"Looks like."

"That puts your Spread Eagle inside Mexico," Jess said and Riker looked at him glumly. They rode on for another full minute in silence. Then Riker said, "I think the old man wants one more crack at El Lupo. Will you go along, Bogan?"

"The deal's a little different from what it was in Holtville," Jess said, weighing his words carefully.

"The hell it is!"

"The hell it isn't. Barthen's on Ortega's land. He sleeps in Ortega's house. . . ."

"Forget I asked you," Riker snapped, pulled his horse away and caught up with Barthen and Smith. The three of them then began to discuss their plans, and from time to time Smith looked back over his shoulder at Jess, his thin face disdainful.

"What's the trouble?" Bill Crown said, coming up alongside Bogan.

'Spread Eagle just got its left wing clipped," Jess told him. "Ben Barthen made a wrong guess."

"You mean this war's over? No more paydays?"

Jess smiled without humor. "I think they're going to give you one more," he said. "Maybe even sweeten the pot for you."

"You say that," Crown said, "like you're folding your own hand."

"I am," Jess said, then swung his head north, to the strange sight of a saddled but riderless horse loping toward them.

"Well, looka yonder," Crown said a moment later.

"Race you to it, Bogan—winner take all!" The two gun-fighters veered toward the stray, Crown going hell-for-leather to claim the prize, Jess not all that interested. Crown dipped low, scooped up the trailing reins expertly and came to a halt.

"Hey!" he said then. "This is a Spread Eagle bronc!"

It sure was, Jess agreed, eyeing the brand.

"Pretty beat-up saddle," Crown said. "Don't belong to nobody I know."

Jess was looking at the ancient piece of leather himself, the worn saddlebags. He lifted the flap, reached down inside for some kind of identification. His searching fingers suddenly touched something very familiar—painfully familiar as he brought back the pouch that he had carried to Branch Arnett from the mountain.

"What's the matter, Bogan?"

"This belongs to a friend of mine," he said, dropping the pouch into his shirt pocket. "I got to follow his back-trail."

"That ain't Conerley's saddle?"

Jess shook his head. "A kind of third partner. Tell Riker, will you?"

"You can tell him yourself," Crown said. "Here he comes."

Jess turned to the oncoming foreman.

"What's this?" Riker said. "By God, one of ours!"

"Ridden by Branch Arnett," Jess said quietly.

"Mary's granddad?" The ramrod looked stricken. "But he's a ranchhand. What's he doing so far from the spread?"

"A little errand up in Westmoreland."

"But Holtville's between here and Westmoreland."

Jess nodded. "That's where I'm headed. . . ."

"That's where we're headed," Riker said. "Let's ride!"

"Need any more help?" Crown volunteered.

"Come on," Riker told him. The three men broke north at a hard gallop and the ground passed swiftly beneath the pounding hooves. Two of the riders felt an urgency for speed. The third was just earning his pay. But it was Crown, nevertheless, whose sharp eyes spotted the swaying figure hanging from a tree in the distance.

Jess Bogan cut the lynched body of his friend down, laid it gently on the ground and covered it with his blanket until a grave could be dug.

"Smoke!" Fran Riker suddenly shouted, pointing to the thin wisp of gray curling above the treetops further north. "That's Mary's place!"

Now they rode even harder—two of them with cold dread gripping their hearts, the third mystified but caught up in the feeling that something very bad was happening. Or already had.

As they neared the little ranch the smoke grew thicker. Then they could see the outbuildings aflame, the dry grass burning, and tongues of fire licking from the windows of the sad little house.

"Mary!" Fran Riker cried agonizingly when they were still fifty yards away. *"Mary!"*

He and Bogan all but threw themselves from their horses and plunged shoulder-to-shoulder into the blazing building. From room to room they went, heedless of the fire burning all around them, emerged with eyes red and smarting, faces streaked with soot, clothes scorched. But with new hope. The girl was not in that inferno.

"They'd head in this direction," Jess said, pointing southwesterly.

"And only fifteen minutes headstart," Riker agreed.

And winded though their animals were they responded to this third demand for headlong speed. Five minutes went by at that pace. Ten. But no sign of any attacking party. Riker abruptly raised his hand, reined in. When he turned to Bogan his expression was ragged with doubt.

"You must've figured their direction wrong," he said wretchedly. "We'd have spotted some sign by now."

Jess shook his head. "They wouldn't roam any further north," he said, "and we came from due south. Let's keep going this way. . . ."

"No! They've gone west. Maybe they're not even with Ortega. There's lots of stray bandits roaming this country."

"I stick to this route," Bogan said again.

"Then good luck to you!" Riker shouted half-wildly, swung his horse right and rode off.

"Never saw that man come unstrung before," Bill

Crown commented. "Who we looking for, anyhow?"

"A girl," Jess said. "Quite a girl. You coming this way?"

"Stringin' right along, boy. Let's go!"

It wasn't the direction that had been wrong but the time allowance. Ten minutes later they spied a group of sombreroed riders a half-mile ahead. As they closed the gap Bogan counted six, and in their midst the female they had captured.

Oh, Riker, I could use you now, Jess thought.

Then they were spotted by the raiders and there was a great waving of rifles, shouts and confusion among them.

"Whatta you say, boy?" Crown asked him. "Do we dog the bastards till sundown, or rush 'em?"

"Let's blow 'em down, Bill!" Jess said recklessly, choosing the handgun over the rifle in its boot. Up ahead, defensive action was being taken. Four of the Mex wheeled on their magnificent little mustangs, strung themselves out across the trail and in the brush on either side. The other two raced off with Mary, one of them urging her bigger, slower horse on with thong lashes across the animal's loins.

"My two are on the left," Crown yelled.

"Take 'em!"

The Mexicans opened fire—even though the range was a long three hundred feet. That was their custom and no one was ever going to teach them different. Crown and Bogan bore in, bodies jackknifed across the withers, gave no answers with their own .45's Not yet. The distance narrowed by the second. Two hundred feet, one hundred. Now the Mexican slugs had a whine to them as they passed by, an angry buzz. Eighty feet. Sixty.

Jess had picked his target from the beginning of the charge. So had Crown. And without so much as a glance at each other the two who made their living with a gun let go, almost in the same instant. The Mexicans blocking the trail itself were blown clear from their saddles. Then Crown had a nasty accident. From the brush came a slug that snapped a tendon in his horse's foreleg. The animal pitched downward and its rider was hurtled six feet through the air to land on his collarbone.

GUNS OF REVENGE

Bogan abandoned his own brush quarry to cover Crown, sent a withering fire to the left even as he was reaching across his body to unboot the Winchester. Crown, somehow, was still conscious. Very. He ran to his fallen horse, slipped his own rifle free and poured a stream of deadly lead to the right. The exchange had been made without a second's hesitation, without a lost motion, and the result was two more dead Mex.

"See you down the road, Bill!" Jess called to him then, racing off in pursuit of the other pair, leaving Crown to do what he had to do for his own doomed horse and grab a new one.

The two up ahead had glanced over their shoulders and seen what had happened to their trailblock. That and the slowness of the girl's genteel dobbin was giving them a lot to think about.

"Basta por mio!" cried one, raking the mustang with his heels and taking off for the hills. Enough for him.

His companion watched the yardage open up and debated furiously. To flee and live? Life, after all, was sweet. But how much sweeter with this white-skinned *rubio* to warm his blankets tonight. . . .

He darted a look behind. The oncoming Bogan looked like God's own vengeance—and coming closer with every breath. He stared ahead and his companion was fast disappearing. With a growl of frustrated rage he lashed his arm out at the helplessly wrist-bound girl, knocked her sprawling from the saddle and into the brush. Then, whipping his own horse with a frenzy, he fled for safety.

Bogan had to watch it and he groaned, felt his stomach tighten and the blood pound against his temples. The murderous impulse was to chase the sonofabitch down and beat him senseless. Compassion and good sense made him pull up sharply and go to Mary's aid. She lay face down and unconscious in the harsh undergrowth. Bogan got his long, strong hands beneath her, rolled her gently into his arms and lifted her out of there. Bill Crown came riding up.

"Hell, boy, she ain't dead?" he asked anxiously.

Jess shook his head. "Not bleeding, either,' he said with relief.

97

"Want me to take off after the scudders?"

"Not alone, no."

The dark-haired Crown peered down into Mary's up-turned face. "That's some nice looking girl," he commented expertly. His glance went along the limp figure in Jess' arms. "What're we goin' to do with her, you reckon?"

"Trying to figure," Jess said. "That was the last of her folks we found lynched back there. And that was her home we found burning down. I don't know what to do."

"Stash her down to Spread Eagle," Crown said. "I hear they got ten, twelve bedrooms in the big house. Can you imagine?"

"No," Jess said. He didn't think much of that idea. Not if Ben Barthen was going to try to hang onto Spread Eagle come hell or high water. Take the girl back up to Holt-ville, then? If this was gold in the pouch he was carrying there'd be enough to tide her over for a spell. He reached around her into his shirt, lifted out the sack and dropped it into the pocket of the dress she was wearing.

"What is that, anyhow?" Crown asked.

"I'm hoping it's gold," Jess said, ready to confide any-thing to this standfast. Talk about a man to ride with . . .

"Gold? Well, say! Where'd you come by it?"

"Scratched it out of a mountain south of here. Me and Beau."

Crown gazed down at him. "Don't suppose you'd . . . No, a man'd have to be crazy to do that."

"Welcome to half of my share, you want to work your-self half to death getting it out of the rock," Jess told him. "Only a sixth interest."

"Who else is partners?"

"Me and Beau and—Mary, here."

"Sure like to get in on it," Crown said.

"Done," Jess said. "Now, partner, what're we going to do with one of the big owners?"

"You don't like taking her down to the *hacienda?*"

"Not much. How about doubling back to the town?"

They both looked up the trail at the sound of the fast-approaching hoofbeats. It was Fran Riker. His face looked stricken as he slammed his horse to a halt, slid from the saddle and rushed to Bogan and the limp figure he held effortlessly in his arms. The Spread Eagle foreman stared beseechingly into Bogan's eyes and Jess smiled reassuringly.

"Just got the wind knocked out of her," he said. "Damn Mex swiped her just before he took off."

"Here, let me take her," Riker said and took charge possessively. Bogan made the transfer without comment. The movement made the girl stir and her eyelids fluttered. Then, with a soft moan, her eyes opened, focused on the face of Fran Riker directly above. A moment later memory flooded back into her conscious mind—the bandits swarming into the yard, forcing their way into the house, being dragged outside and forced to mount the horse. The leering faces, suggestive voices, the ones with the torches running around like madmen. The wild ride with them in the direction of the border. The sudden consternation from something that had suddenly appeared in the rear . . .

The remembering first, then the realization that she was being carried in Fran Riker's arms, that, by some miracle, she had been saved from the one experience a woman fears more than even the taking of her life . . .

She reached up her arms and entwined them around Riker's neck, laid her face against his chest.

Oh, Fran!" she murmured. *"Fran!"*

Riker looked across the top of her head at Bogan and his face was a strange, expressionless mask. Bill Crown glanced down at both men and read the situation accurately. No one, for many long seconds, spoke, and the only sound was the soft, relieved crying of the girl.

"I'll take you down to the spread," Riker said then. "You'll be safe there." He looked over again at Bogan. "You coming, mister?"

"To collect my gear," Jess said and mounted up. He swung his horse northeasterly.

"Where you headed, Jess?" Crown asked him.

"Going to bury the old man," Bogan answered.

"Give you a hand," Crown said and the two of them rode off from Riker and the grateful girl in his arms. Night had fallen when they reached the ranch again and Jess finished his supper quickly, went to the bunkhouse where he found Beau staring thoughtfully at the ceiling.

"Ready to pull out of here, kid?" he asked and was surprised at the look Conerley gave him.

"Got my walkin' papers, did I?"

Jess shook his head, puzzled. "Why should you? What happened?"

"Oh, not much," Beau said, and then the familiar sheepish smile appeared. "I just got caught romancin', is all."

"Caught by who?"

"The husband. Had to rough him up a mite."

Bogan frowned down at him. "Couldn't leave her alone, could you?"

"Leave *her* alone?" Conerley protested. "Hell's bells, Jess, that gal came right up to the bunkhouse door dressed like an El Paso whore. Ask any of the boys." He turned his head to the four cardplayers in the rear. "Listen—any one of you done different than me this afternoon?"

"She got what she come for," said one.

"Only me," said another, "I'd've shared her with my old bunkmates." There was general laughter.

"All right, all right," Bogan told Conerley gruffly. "Now we got two reasons to drift."

"What's yours?"

"This ain't the holy crusade it used to be," Jess told him. "El Lupo's in the right and Barthen is wrong."

"How come?"

"It's his land, that's how come."

"What difference does that make?" Beau asked. "He's only a Mex, ain't he?"

"And we're two raggedy pants gunmen. Where the hell do we come off stealing anybody's property, even if it belongs to Mex?"

"Well, you put it that way, Jess, and it changes some. One thing I ain't is a thief. Where we bound for, buddy?"

The bunkhouse door swung open and the fighter named Wightman put his head inside.

"Everybody up to the main house," he told them. "Big powwow." His glance fell on Jess. "Riker sent a special invite to you, Bogan. Says you and your sidekick owe Spread Eagle one more ride."

Jess looked at the man but thought of Riker. He had

an idea what he meant about him and Beau 'owing' Spread Eagle.

"All right," he said. "I'll be along."

3

Ben Barthen was so used to the habit of success, of making the right guess, that his mind was not flexible enough to admit that this time he had blundered on a big scale. The venture into this country had been calculated to be costly. Opposition had been anticipated. But all his plans had been made with the natural assumption that he would succeed—and the vast profits would quickly absorb the initial losses.

But if the Lieutenant was right, if the official border was to be some ten miles north of here, then the whole scheme had failed and he might never recoup. Except that Ben Barthen could not fail, and therefore the Lieutenant was wrong. Let the damn army pull back to El Centro. This, right here, was Spread Eagle, and the time had come to smash the opposition once and for all.

That had been Cyril Smith's idea this afternoon, and now Fran Riker no longer opposed it—although Riker's private reasons for attacking El Lupo were somewhat defeatist. He wanted the Mexican force reduced so that the major part of the herd could be salvaged. The foreman had no illusions about Spread Eagle maintaining itself in Mexican territory.

The three men had suppered together in the main house and were making the final preparations when young Carl Barthen came into the room. He held himself stiffly, sullenly, but what caught their attention most was the ugly bluish welt along one pale jaw.

"What happened, Carl?"

The son told his father. Told the story simply, calmly, graphically, and when he was through Fran Riker came to his feet, turned to Ben Barthen.

"I'll have Conerley brought in here," he said. "We can try him and hang him before we leave."

"No," Carl said. "The man's no more guilty than my wife."

101

"Which is probably true," Ben Barthen said acidly. "Besides that, we have need for every gun on the ranch tonight."

"I wouldn't count on Conerley, boss. He'll probably side with Bogan—" Riker's voice broke off as a thought occurred to him. "This Bogan and his damn principles," he said. "What happened here this afternoon might be the lever I need. Suppose I call the crew in and we get this thing started?"

"Right. Let's get this thing going."

Riker went out of the room.

"Father, I want to go along with the men," Carl said then.

"Don't be ridiculous. There's going to be a gunfight out there."

"That's why I want to go. I have to find out about myself."

Barthen looked at his son closely, saw that Carl was not making idle bravado. He really did want to prove himself. Ben nodded.

"All right, Carl. But better change into something dark. And on the bureau in my bedroom you'll find a new Colt."

Carl went upstairs, entered his own room. Miriam lay on the bed, her eyes closed, and as Carl changed into a dark shirt and levis he tried not to look at her, at the expanse of white thigh where the robe was parted.

"Where are you going?" she asked, startling him.

"They're riding against the Mexicans. I'm going with them."

"Is he going, too?"

Carl let out a breath. "I expect so," he said. "That's what he gets paid to do."

"But you're going to fight for nothing?"

"Not exactly nothing, Miriam."

"You're going to show me, is that it?"

"I stopped thinking about you this afternoon."

She raised one leg, bent the knee and the robe fell away.

"I'll be right here when you get back, Carl."

"It's all over," he said tightly. "You're leaving in the morning."

"All right," she told him. "But I'll still be here tonight." Carl left her quickly.

In another part of the house, Fran Riker was looking in on Mary Washen. At his direction supper had been served to her in the room and now she was finishing.

"How do you feel, Mary?"

"Spoiled and pampered, Fran," she told him with a warm smile. "This is the grandest house I've ever seen in my life."

"Little too big for my tastes," he said. "And for my salary. Though," he added quickly, "I don't expect to work for another man much longer now."

"You'll have your own ranch?"

"Someday," he said. "Someday when Spread Eagle's troubles are settled."

"But there's still more fighting to be done?"

He nodded. "Things are coming to a head here, Mary. One way or another. But there's something else I came to tell you about. Something rather unhappy, I'm afraid."

"What is it?"

"Before those raiders attacked your place," he said, "they met up with your grandfather . . ."

"Oh, no!"

"Yes," Riker said. "He's gone, Mary."

"I—I can't believe it," she said. "I've been sitting here thinking about him, hoping to see him."

"He was on some errand for Bogan," Riker said. "Some business matter."

"The gold," she said, reaching into the pocket of her dress and taking out the sack she had unexplainedly found there.

"What gold?" Riker asked, staring at the leather pouch.

"Gramps knew about some mountain," Mary said. "He told Jess Bogan about it and Jess found it. This is a sample of what he mined."

"So that's their big business venture," Riker said. "And your granddad was going to have it assayed in Westmoreland . . ."

"But how did it arrive in my pocket?" she started to ask, then realization dawned. "Why, Jess must have put it there," she said. "But when?"

103

"I don't know," Riker said, his voice low.

"And that's something else I've been thinking about," Mary said then. "They were along to help you today, Jess and the other man?"

"Yes, they were along."

"And I never thanked them," she said contritely. "I was so overwhelmed to be saved that I never told them how grateful I was."

"I'll relay your thanks," Riker said, and the girl looked at him with some surprise.

"I'd like to tell them myself," she said. "That would be all right, wouldn't it, Fran?"

"Not now, Mary. They've both got work to do tonight."

"Gunfighting?"

"Work," Riker repeated. "What they get paid good wages for."

"Well, in the morning then," she said.

"In the morning," Riker said. "I'll have something I want to say to you in the morning, too."

"All right, Fran," she said. "But please be careful in this *work* you have to do tonight. All of you be careful."

"We will. Good night, Mary, and have a good rest."

Riker left the room and went downstairs to where the guncrew was assembling. He caught Jess Bogan's eye and signaled him to follow to an anteroom for a private talk. They stood and faced each other with open hostility between them.

"How is Mary?" Jess asked.

"I just left her and she's fine," Riker said stiffly. "She sends her gratitude to you and Crown."

"Oh?" Jess said, his glance quizzical. But the foreman shook his head.

"No," he said brusquely, "I haven't told her. And regardless of what your opinion of me is, my reasons are for the best for all concerned."

"That remains to be seen."

"No, Bogan. Between the two of us there is only one right man for Mary. I am that man. You're going to ride for this outfit one more time. By morning you'll be gone from Spread Eagle."

"Sound pretty positive, mister."

104

GUNS OF REVENGE

"I am. And I'll tell you why. You signed on here with a man you acknowledged as your partner. This afternoon your partner committed adultery with the daughter-in-law of the man who pays your wages. Without much persuasion that charge could also be changed to rape. In any event," Riker said coldly, "your partner is liable to whatever justice the owner of Spread Eagle wants to hand him. Do you recognize Ben Barthen's rights about that?"

"Yes," Jess said slowly. In this situation Barthen was the law. No denying it.

"My first inclination," Riker said, "was to advise the owner to hang Conerley. My second thought was to make the both of you an offer. You ride with the crew against El Lupo tonight. You clear out by morning. The matter pending against Conerley will be considered settled. Well?"

It was what Jess had been expecting and now he nodded his head.

"We'll give you a ride, Riker."

"And be gone from here afterward," the foreman said insistently. "No attempt to see or talk to Mary Washen."

Jess smiled sadly. "Right now," he said, "you must hate your own guts."

Riker's eyes blazed and his body tensed. It looked as if he would fight.

"Let's get inside to the meeting," he said instead, turning his face abruptly from the searching, unrelenting gaze of Bogan. Jess followed him inside, and when he saw Carl Barthen there with a shiny new Colt at his hip he frowned darkly.

This he didn't like at all. Ben Barthen might find it practical to drop the thing against Beau—but would his son be willing to forget it? *Damn Beau, anyhow. Damn the whole sorry mess. . . .*

Cyril Smith had the floor, his eyes glittering feverishly in his pinched face as he explained the attack that he, Barthen and Riker had decided upon. They would leave the ranch in groups of two, spaced five minutes apart so as not to alarm any possible scouting patrols sent out by El Lupo. They would rendezvous at the southern end of the pine grove, then form into two parties. One would

105

work around to the west opening of the canyon and at Smith's signal strike up a heavy fire into that mouth. Coming from this direction, the Mex would presume it to be soldiers and that they were outnumbered. They would, according to the Englishman, pour out the east mouth— where the second group from Spread Eagle would be waiting for them.

"The first group, meanwhile," Smith finished, "will be pressing the attack upon the enemy's rear. Gentlemen, it will be shooting fish in a barrel."

The hell it will, Bogan thought. There'll be so much going on out there that they'll end up killing each other. He wondered how Riker could have endorsed such a desperate stunt. He found Riker watching him closely, and then the foreman was moving toward him, speaking in an undertone when he got there.

"What do you think, Bogan?" he asked and there was a frank appeal in his voice, an appeal to postpone their other differences for the time being.

"What do I think? I think Barthen wants to take a few scalps for his own goddamn pride. He's licked and he won't admit it."

"We might get away with it."

"And what if you do? You can't stay on this range."

"But I can get my beef back safe," Riker said.

"Oh," Jess said. "Now I see your angle."

"No," Riker said. "Now you see my job. I don't run gunfighters, Bogan. I'm a cattleman, first, last and always."

"Why not dicker for your beeves?"

The foreman shook his head. "You don't know Ben Barthen. He wouldn't dicker with God to get into heaven."

"And that's that," Jess said, his voice resigned. "But what about the son over there? What's he doing with a gun?"

Riker sighed. "I hear he's riding with us. Going to prove himself to the old man."

"Keep him away from Beau, then," Jess warned. "I'm committed to this fool play, but I won't be responsible for any private arguments."

"I don't like it any more than you do, Bogan," Riker said. "At least we're agreed on something."

GUNS OF REVENGE

"Yeah," Jess said. Then Riker touched his arm, very briefly.

"It's too bad," he said. "About us, I mean. I wish you'd never have met Mary that night."

"I don't, Jess said. "And I don't think you're the man for her . . ."

Then Ben Barthen was approaching them, his hand outstretched to Jess, wishing him a safe return, murmuring vaguely about a bonus. He shook the hands of all the men who were going out to do his fighting for him, even Beau Conerley's.

They left the house then, mounted up, and Smith paired them off, reveling in his own importance. Bogan drew Crown and was assigned to the second group at the rendezvous. Beau was assigned with Rowe, also in the second group.

"I knew if I led a clean life I'd get the easy jobs," Crown said as he and Jess led off.

"What's it like, friend, shooting fish in a barrel?"

"Damned if I've found out yet. But that's what the straw boss is always tellin' me just before hell busts loose."

"Always was and always will," Bogan said.

"At least they didn't send a bunch of punchers along on this outing. Damn, I get to worrying more about them innocents in a scrap than my own self."

Bogan was grateful for that himself, although he knew that Riker had his own reason for holding the cowmen back. Even now they were riding through patches of the stock, a herd strung out god-knew-where, left practically on its own—and Jess didn't envy the ranch crew their round-up. If and when Spread Eagle got out from under the threat of Ortega.

Tonight Crown led him on a straightaway route to the pine grove and they arrived at the rendezvous after an hour's steady travel. The others assembled at prescribed intervals and then Smith, growing more officious and irritating by the minute, led the diversionary party in single file around the slope of the curiously peaceful-looking canyon wall. Riker posted his sharpshooters at the eastern opening, set himself behind a large rock cropping in the center.

107

"This looks too damn easy, Jess," Beau Conerley said suspiciously.

"You mean cause there ain't a sentry, kid?"

"Yeh, that's it. We should've seen some Mex."

A barrage of shooting broke sharply through the night's quiet. Wild shouting. Bogan rested on one knee, the carbine at his shoulder. There was another flurry of firing, more yelling. Bogan looked over at Conerley, at Riker, marked the tenseness in them as they waited for that outpouring of Mexicans. All at once a great sound of laughing poured out of him. The big man stood erect, roaring with laughter.

"For crissake, Jess!"

"Wait, Beau," Jess told him, choking back the laughter. "Just wait and see."

There was a third fusillade, half-hearted-sounding, and no shouting at all. Then the voice of Cyril Smith, sharp and piercing from within the canyon itself.

"Hold your fire, Riker!" it commanded nervously. "The bloody scoundrel has flown the coop!"

Sure enough, El Lupo had fled. That he and a sizable force had been there, and recently, was plain enough from the remains of campfires, the trod-down earth, the very look of the place. Bogan walked through the canyon, emerged at the far end, listening all the while to the Englishman's shrill accusations.

"He was warned, Riker! There can't be any doubt of it! This happened at the Khyber Pass. There's an informer in our ranks!"

"You think so, Jess?" Beau asked.

"I think El Lupo plays it by the book," Bogan said. "He sent three men out this morning and got none back. So he moved."

"In the saddle, Spread Eagle!" Smith was crying at the top of his voice. "Mount up! The General ran because he fears us!" The Englishman was having trouble with his own mount. It kept circling skittishly. "The Mex is afraid, men! Now is our time to root him out, cut him to ribbons!"

As if those fearless words were a signal, El Lupo's 'frightened' band launched their own attack. They seemed

108

to rise up out of the dark ground, fifty shrieking, shooting men on fifty low charging horses—and there wasn't a point on the compass that the blaze of their guns didn't fill.

"Fall back, fall back!" Smith screamed. "Into the canyon!"

The hell with that, Bogan thought, going flat on his belly, thinking better of his chances here than bottled up tight between those craggy walls. So did Crown and Mc-Crillus, who slid from their horses and lay prone among the jutting rocks.

"Get down here, Beau!" Jess shouted at the still-mounted, undecided-looking Conerley. "It's your best chance, kid!"

"Into the canyon, into the canyon!" Smith was ranting. Conerley broke that way, became one with the group rushing to get inside. Then the first wave of attackers rolled over them. This was life or death, and when Bogan aimed the carbine now it was to kill. He fired at point-blank range, drove a man from his saddle. Crown took another. McCrillus scored, knocking the howling Mex almost on top of Bogan. The fellow came up on his knees, still full of fight, and Jess knocked him senseless.

The three of them took eight attackers out of the battle in a wild half-minute, effectively blocking the assault from that quarter, and in the thick of the melee a strong Mexican voice could be clearly heard barking orders.

"Los eviten, los eviten! El canon atacen!" Avoid the ones out here! Attack the canyon! His men instantly wheeled, changed direction. Bogan thought he got one, was certain that another fell from Crown's unerring rifle. Seconds later all the fighting was going on at their backs, at both ends of the canyon as Ortega concentrated everything he had on a quick knockout of Spread Eagle's main force sealed inside there.

"What's it gonna be, Bogan? Run or commit suicide?"

"Let's open up that far side."

"I'm with you, buster!"

They all three began running, bodies crouched low, skirting the battle at this end with plenty to spare and coming up behind the other Mexicans.

109

"Spread ourselves thin and pour it on fast," Bogan said. "We got to get on their nerves more than anything else."

It was a guess and a gamble that this part of Ortega's force thought they had all their enemies in front of them —and Bogan knew it had paid off almost with the first barrage laid down. Three fell, but the immediate consternation of the other twenty was the real result. He, Crown and McCrillus let go with another round almost immediately. Half a dozen guns answered, but by now the realization was forming that it was they who might be caught in the middle. Bogan and company peppered away a third time. El Lupo's ranks broke in confusion, horses went bounding off at right angles to the line of fire, leaving the canyon mouth open except for the dead and wounded.

"Break out, Spread Eagle!" Bogan shouted encouragingly. "Run for it!"

There were no immediate takers. Then three riders burst from that death trap, a fourth—their figures indistinguishable in the night.

"Beau!" Jess called. "Over here, Beau!" But Conerley didn't appear, and now the horsemen pouring out of the canyon mouth were the other half of Ortega's raiders. There was a great confusion.

"Come on, Bogan!" Crown yelled in his ear. "What in hell are you waitin' on?" Ortega's men were fanning out, preparing to encircle them.

"You see my partner anywhere?"

"All I see are Mexicans! For crissake, boy, let's *git!*"

The three of them dashed back the way they had come, for their precious horses. Wild Mexican voices were shouting all around them, gunfire all but ringed them in and bullets filled the air like hailstones in a storm. Bogan found his horse and had it running when he himself had but one boot in the stirrup.

"This way!" Crown was yelling from his own mount. "There's a gap in the line this way!" They broke for the hole in the fast-closing circle, slammed through the opening with their own guns blazing murderously. They went through the Mexican line and kept on going directly south, into the wilder country, made the pursuit of them more

110

and more discouraging by the accuracy of their shooting. Then the chase was over and they began to work their way back northeast.

"Any of us hurt?" Bogan asked into the sweet, peaceful quiet they had now.

The word-saving McCrillus merely grunted and Bill Crown found relief in a laugh. "Ain't hurt," he said, "but this dog knows he had his tail in a crick!"

"Real close," Jess agreed.

"And some friggin' strategy that Smith dreamed up," Crown said. "Some fish in a barrel they turned out to be."

Jess said nothing. He had been denying it and denying it to himself for the past quarter hour now, but the bitterness in Crown's voice somehow made a certainty of the thing. Beau was dead.

3

Beau Conerley, Joe Tanney and Carl Barthen were among the missing. Three other riders bore wounds from the debacle but they had made it back to the ranch.

Fran Riker was one of them. Spread Eagle's foreman had stopped a slug that fractured his kneecap. Not a mortal injury, certainly, but a crippling one that kept him confined to a bed and out of the main stream of events at the ranch. Ben Barthen ordered him moved into the *hacienda* and Mary came to be his nurse and offer what comfort she could.

But the man was inconsolable, almost unapproachable. He had been in on the original planning of the attack, and though he had not shared the enthusiasm of the other two about its success, still he had voiced his approval, lent his supposedly good judgment. Salvaging the herd, after all, was his prime responsibility to Ben Barthen—and cutting down Ortega's forces had seemed the best way to get that valuable beef back to the home ranch.

And then to run into the humiliating beating they had taken tonight. . . .

"Try to sleep, Fran," Mary told him softly, smoothing her cool fingers across his fevered brow. "You have to get your strength back."

111

He looked up into her beautiful face. Suddenly his eyes widened.

"What is it, Fran? What are you staring at?"

"Nothing," he said, shaking his head. That seemed to make the hallucination disappear—the strange vision he'd had of Jess Bogan gazing down at him over Mary's shoulder. Bogan, whose judgment had stood up twice this fateful day. *No,* the man told himself stubbornly. *No. This girl is mine. I am the only man worthy of her. . . .*

"Mary, there was something I was going to ask you in the morning. Something very important."

Her face showed she knew what is was. His proposal. And she knew what she was going to answer this man who had saved her this afternoon. Knew what it was, but didn't want to give it tonight. The why of that escaped her. She simply didn't want to tell him she would marry him until tomorrow. It had something to do with seeing Jess Bogan once more without being promised to another man. To see him and thank him for helping Fran in what they had done for her. . . .

"Ask me in the morning," she said aloud. "When the sun is shining through your window."

"No," Riker said. "Now. Mary, will you marry me?"

The girl's eyes closed and opened and she sighed deeply. Then she nodded.

"Yes," she said in a small voice. "I'll marry you."

He took her hand, grasped it firmly. "Because I'm the only man for you?" he asked. "Because of what I'm going to make of myself?"

"Yes," she said vaguely. "I suppose. But mostly because you showed me how much I mean to you. Because you risked your life without hesitation to save mine."

Riker studied her very thoughtfully, said nothing.

"Now you must try to sleep, Fran. We have a lot to talk about in the morning."

The man nodded, turned his face on the pillow and closed his eyes.

The other wounded riders had been carried into the bunkhouse where the wrangler treated them in his rough fashion. Cyril Smith, still jaunty, still affecting the manner of a field marshal, visited them there. All the assembled crew was surprised to hear from the Englishman that they had scored a tremendous victory over El Lupo tonight.

"We took on the best he had, men," Smith announced, "and hurt him badly. I daresay he lost half his forces in the engagement, and the rest are still running . . ."

A deep, ominous growl broke into his speech.

"Mister," Bill Crown said, "why don't you get to hell out of here?"

Smith's head popped erect. "And who do you think you're talking to?" he demanded shrilly.

"I'm talkin' to the stupid sonofabitch that dragged these boys into a rat hole tonight and left three of them behind. And if we'd all listened to you raving out there none of us would've made it back alive. Now get out of my sight!"

"That's insubordination, b'God!" Smith cried. "I'll report your infernal insolence to Mr. Barthen immediately!"

There was a derisive guffaw from the room at that.

"Beat it," Crown said, "before I put you down with the rest of the privy rats."

"Hey, you gunfighters!" an excited voice called from outside. "There's a Mex out here!" McCrillus was the first one through the door, gun in hand, but the weapon would not be necessary. The Mexican was a smooth-faced youngster, not more than seventeen, and unarmed. He rode a frisky horse and carried a white flag of truce attached to an army guidon.

The gun crew came out of the bunkhouse and surveyed the boy curiously.

"What can we do for you?" Bogan asked in Spanish.

"I speak your language, hombre," the boy said proudly, with only a trace of accent.

Smith pushed his way in front of Jess.

"Well? What is it?" he demanded importantly.

"Where is *Señor* Barthen?" the boy asked. "I have a message for the meester boss from the General."

"Aha!" Smith crowed. "Does he sue for peace?"

The boy looked down at him disdainfully. "You," he said with great scorn, "are *El Ingles*. I want *Señor* Barthen only."

Ben Barthen emerged from the shadows, walking

slowly, his face saddened by the night's hard news.

"I'm the boss," he said tonelessly. "What do you want?"

The messenger inspected Barthen now, then took a folded paper from his shirt and handed it to him. Barthen opened it, saw that it was written in Spanish and passed it over to Smith.

"Read it aloud, Major," he said.

"It's from the bloody Ortega right enough," Smith said. " 'Sir,' " he read, " 'I have your son as my prisoner. He is alive but in some pain from a wound in the side. I offer him safe return to you in exchange for—' " Smith stopped reading abruptly.

"Go on, man, go on!" Barthen told him.

" '. . . in exchange for the Englishman . . . named Cyril Smith . . . who is an escaped prisoner of the Mexican Government . . . and under sentence of death . . .' " Smith's voice trailed away and he would have torn the message in two had not Bogan taken it from his fingers.

Jess read the rest of the note to himself. '. . . under sentence of death for cowardice and desertion in battle. This exchange of prisoners will take place on the banks of the Rio Blanco, approximately five kilometers from the Casa del Ortega which you temporarily hold, and within two hours of the time my messenger leaves you. Otherwise, your son will be executed in place of the Englishman.' It was signed with a large, flourishing letter 'O', similar, Jess reflected, to the large monogram set in the stone courtyard of the ranch.

"He wants the swap made in two hours," Bogan said aloud to Ben Barthen. "On the banks of the Rio Blanco."

There followed a very heavy and uncomfortable silence. Smith finally broke it.

"Ortega is lying," he said in a thin voice. "I was beside Carl when he went down. Shot through the heart, Mr. Barthen."

"No," the young Mex said. *El Ingles* lies. The son of meester boss is not dead . . ."

"It's a trick!" Smith protested shrilly. "The dirty murdering swine wants me at any cost. I know too much about his conduct of the war . . ."

Barthen held up his hand and Smith fell quiet.

114

GUNS OF REVENGE

"Tell Ortega that the exchange is unacceptable," he said to the messenger. "But tell him that for the life of my son I will evacuate this ranch at dawn—leave the cattle, everything."

The boy's thin shoulders shrugged eloquently. "The General will have all that in any event, *señor*," he said, his young voice matter-of-fact. "For your son he will trade only this man here. Those are my instructions."

Barthen passed a hand wearily over his eyes, shook his head. "I can't," he said very softly. "I can't do a thing like that."

"But we can hang onto you, by God!" Smith said suddenly, reaching up to pull the boy out of the saddle. Both Bogan and Crown were on him together, breaking his grip and jerking him away.

"He carries a truce flag, damnit!" Jess growled. "What kind of soldier are you, anyhow?"

"But we can use him for the exchange! He might be very close to Ortega—"

"I thought Barthen's son was finished," Crown broke in. "Didn't you say that, mister?"

"Yes, yes! But suppose I was mistaken?"

"In that case," Crown reasoned, "go down to the river yourself."

"I must say you're free and easy with my life . . ."

"Stop it, stop it," Barthen said tiredly, then raised his head to the rider. "Go on back to Ortega, boy. My offer to pull stakes still stands."

The Mexican looked extremely sad. "Your offer will be refused," he said. "But that is up to you. I tell you one thing—Ortega would not let his son be hanged in place of this low coward." He touched the brim of his sombrero, wheeled the mount around and started off. Some fifty feet away he stopped. "I know that, meester boss," he called back, "because I am the son of Ortega!" With that he put the horse to a run and was gone from sight.

"Mr. Barthen," Smith said then, "if I thought there was the slightest chance that Carl was alive I'd go there and make the exchange. You do believe me, don't you?"

"Yes, of course," Barthen said absently. "Tell me, why does that man want you so badly?"

115

"For a scapegoat," Smith answered. "With me dead, his own guilt will be buried. His scandalous defeat will be forgotten."

"Is there a map of this range anywhere?" Bogan broke in.

"There's a map on the wall of the study," Barthen answered. "Why?"

"I'd like to look at it."

"You'd be wasting your time," the owner said. "El Lupo has a thousand hiding places out there."

"I didn't figure to track him down—just have a look at the lay of the land around Rio Blanco."

"Why build up false hopes, Bogan?" Smith asked him sharply. "You're talking nonsense."

"You just keep your yap shut from here on in," Jess told him, then shifted his gaze to Barthen. "If he kept one prisoner alive," he said, "he may have kept three. I'd like to find out."

Barthen waved him to the house. "Help yourself," he said without enthusiasm.

Bogan started for the *hacienda* and after half a dozen steps sensed he was being followed. He turned to see the square figure of Crown.

"They're dead," the dark-haired man said. "But I'm like you. I want to be sure."

"Come along and welcome."

The roughhewn pair mounted the steps of the house, went in without knocking—then stopped dead in their tracks. Standing above them in a loosely draped robe, half-way down the center staircase, was the sleepy-eyed, touseled-haired Miriam.

"Did you just get back?" she asked drowsily. "Where's Carl?"

"Your husband didn't make it," Crown told her. "Not yet."

"What do you mean?" She awakened perceptibly, descended the stairs.

"He got hung up in a fight," Bogan said gently. "Nobody knows for sure how he made out."

She shook her head. "I can't believe it," she said. "Not Carl. He couldn't—it wasn't in him to fight anyone." The

116

girl smiled, as if these two had been teasing her. "He'll be back," she said. "He's just trying to be dramatic."

"That's right," Bogan said.

"Just so I'll worry," she said, convincing herself. Then, free of concern for her husband, Miriam's face changed. "Everybody else got back, didn't they?" she asked Bogan.

Jess shook his head.

"Beau?" she asked. "Do you know Beau—a fellow with red hair?"

"Not yet for him, either," Jess said, and now she wasn't sure at all that someone was playing a game with her.

"But he will? Beau will come back?"

"You keep hoping," Jess said. "For both of them." There was a note of commiseration in his deep voice and she looked at him candidly.

"I guess you know what happened this afternoon," Miriam said. "I guess the whole ranch knows."

"We came to look at a map, Jess," Crown told him impatiently. "Let's get to it." They both nodded to the somewhat pathetic-looking girl and moved away down the hall toward Barthen's study.

In a room directly above them Mary Washen was checking on her patient.

"Can't you sleep, Fran?" she asked.

"No. I hear a lot of arguing going on outside. What's it all about?"

"I heard it from my room, too," the girl said. "As near as I can make out, Mr. Barthen's son is still alive and Ortega has him."

"He won't be alive for long, then," Riker said pessimistically.

"Well, he sent a messenger to arrange a trade. Or some such thing. Is there a man named Smith here?"

"There sure is."

"That's who Ortega wants to trade for. But apparently Mr. Barthen has refused. Anyhow, they were arguing about it—Jess, especially."

"What's Bogan arguing about?" Riker asked sharply.

"About whether Mr. Barthen's son is really being held

captive or not. The man named Smith says he's dead."

"And Bogan disagrees?"

"Apparently. I heard him ask Mr. Barthen about a map of the area."

Riker laughed harshly. "This time he's wrong," he said, his voice low.

"What did you say, Fran?"

"Bogan's wrong. Barthen's kid is as dead as any other prisoner El Lupo ever took from Spread Eagle. Bogan's just trying a big play to get himself out of the deal we made."

"Deal?" she asked. "What deal, Fran?"

"He agreed to be gone before morning," Riker said, his voice rising angrily. "Now he's stalling for more time."

"I don't understand," she said. "More time for what?"

"To see you!" the wounded man said in agitation. "To tell you—" He broke off abruptly.

"To tell me what?"

"Nothing, Mary. Nothing. I don't even know what I'm talking about."

She settled the blanket over him, rested her hand briefly against his cheek.

"Sleep," she told him. "Sleep and get well for me."

"I will, Mary. I'll be better than new in no time at all."

"Of course you will."

"And remember what I told you—Bogan is wrong about young Barthen. El Lupo kills every Spread Eagle man he can."

Mary, her thoughts troubled by his insistence, said nothing more and left the room.

FIVE

So far as his men were concerned, Don Luis Santos y Ortega would always be the General—and so far as Ortega himself knew, he still was. At any rate, if there were orders de-commissioning him now that the war was officially concluded those papers had been caught up in the great confusion that gripped all of this part of Mexico.

He was a tall, commanding figure, slender as a sword, with dark piercing eyes and a fierce-looking mustache-goatee. Ortega was Spanish-looking rather than Mexican, a man descended from Castilian nobility that had migrated to the New World a century before, assumed title to the land under supposedly inviolable land grants from King Phillip V. His rights still were respected by the Mexican Government, but the disastrous war with America had threatened a whole way of life—and now one particular American was attempting to steal his very home and land.

In that war, as a general commanding an army of his country's troops, Ortega had bent over backwards to treat his enemy with honor. Atrocities by his own men were punished summarily. Atrocities on the other side were regretted. But the new America's strength and spirit had overwhelmed them, their superiority of arms and men had made the last days of the struggle a rout. And until his government sued for peace, Ortega had carried on a brilliant guerilla-type operation that had harried an army three times the size of his own, shredded its supply lines and earned him the respected El Lupo title. The American commanders, in fact, had nothing but a very healthy respect for Luis Ortega with the one exception of his defense of San Jacinto.

Lindgrove, the American Colonel charged with taking the pivotal town, had looked on the assignment gloomily. Its principal defense was a Moorish-type fort, bristling with cannon and all but impregnable walls. The Colonel's intelligence informed him that the fort was plentifully supplied with fresh and eager troops, had ample ammunition and food, and its commander was a supposedly brilliant Englishman, a soldier of fortune named Major Smith.

Lindgrove didn't like it, and all he could do was to surround the impregnable place with his artillery and begin the time-honored siege prescribed in the West Point textbooks. He, too, had ample ammunition—though it dismayed his military heart to throw two-thousand pounds of shell and merely pockmarked those stout walls after forty-eight hours.

119

Then he was stunned to see the white flag of surrender go up just at the time when he was preparing to withdraw. And from the mighty fortress came the strange little Englishman, shaking as if from apoplexy, to hand over San Jacinto and all but conclude the campaign in this section. But as puzzled as Lindgrove was, and grateful, he felt he could not treat the man as a British citizen but had to turn him over to the Provost Marshal as just one more prisoner of the war. That was the last Lindgrove heard of the man and he would have been amused but not surprised to know that Smith had been sentenced to death by a chagrined and angry Mexican government. Good Lord, had Benedict Arnold been guilty of less?

But in the highest places the dishonor of San Jacinto had been smeared across the proud name of Don Luis Ortega. For it was the General who had put his faith in El Ingles, who had assigned him to the defense of the fort with every assurance that even the most mediocre of military talent would be able to hold it indefinitely. As one of the planners of the war, Ortega knew its inevitable end. But even a losing hand has aces, and San Jacinto was to have been the strength from which they would have bargained with the Americans. The new border would be drawn north of the town.

And because of Smith's abject cowardice in battle they had lost twenty thousand square miles of territory.

Small wonder, then, that he wanted the Englishman—that the government wanted him. And small wonder that when Ortega accepted defeat, returned to his home in the deep south, small wonder that he dropped the pretense of war-with-honor at finding an adventurous American flooding his land with cattle, living in his very home, claiming for his own what had been rightfully Ortegas' for over a hundred years.

He looked on Ben Barthen as a thief and fought him as one, with no rules to follow and no holds barred. Then, a week ago, word came that the Englishman had escaped prison, might be trying to make his way out of the country. Five days later there was a report that he had been spotted in the company of two Americans. The scouting party had almost captured him, but the trio made it safely to the army bivouac.

That had been a great disappointment to Luis Ortega—until a spy came in with the amazing news that Cyril Smith was now in league with Barthen. This morning he had handpicked three men, including the invaluable Miguel, sent them to the *hacienda* at dawn for the sole purpose of capturing El Ingles. But they had not returned, and fearing the possibility of ambush, Ortega had prudently pulled his men out of the canyon. Sure enough, the foolish American party had launched a night attack. But Ortega knew now that he had been just as foolish. On hearing the hated voice of Smith ordering his raiders inside the canyon, the General had let himself be blind to everything else but sealing the place off. If he had not bypassed those three outside . . .

Even so, fortune was still with him. He had found two dead within the canyon and one wounded. That one had a pale, almost delicate look to him—and when he proved to be the son of Barthen, Ortega seized on the idea of an exchange. To prove the sincerity of his offer he had sent his own son to make the terms, and now he waited impatiently for Roberto's return.

But when Roberto did arrive at the new camp along the river he brought only disappointment.

"He will not give us *El Ingles, Padre,*" the boy reported.

"Even after he read the message?"

"*El Ingles* read the message. But only a part of it."

"I cannot believe it!" Ortega cried. "The man would have his son hung in place of a criminal?"

"He offered to evacuate our house at dawn."

"Did he? And what did you say to that fine offer?"

"I told him we would take back our house and his cattle regardless."

"And what did he say?"

"Nothing. He seemed quite dejected."

"I am not touched by my enemy's dejection," Luis Ortega said. "Very well. We will keep to our part of the terms exactly. We will move to the appointed spot and wait there for one more hour and thirty minutes."

121

Three of his lieutenants had been listening to the conversation. Now one of them spoke up.

"That is honorable enough, *mi General,* but is it wise to go within five kilometers of them?"

"What can they do, Mario? The river is too wide and too deep for them to risk a crossing at that point. And I want to be very close," he added, "so that if Barthen will not save his son's life he will be sure to see him hanging from the great tree that overlooks the Rio Blanco. All right—move the camp!"

His orders were relayed and soon the force of thirty-five were enroute. In their center, borne on a horsedrawn litter, was Carl Barthen.

2

"What would you say if I backed out of this deal?" Bill Crown asked.

"I'd say that between the two of us there's one brain still working," Bogan told him. The pair had been riding west by south from the ranch for twenty minutes, and if Bogan's map reading was accurate they should reach the Rio Blanco in ten more. Also, if he was accurate, they would reach it a point about a quarter mile north of where Ortega said he would exchange his prisoner.

"But a raft, man!" Crown protested. "The damn thing's gonna tip right over."

"Most likely."

What Crown was worrying about was the crude, makeshift thing their horses were dragging along behind—four rough planks that were more or less lashed between two pine logs.

"Hell, I'd rather take the horses and swim down there," Crown said.

"Me, too. But if we find somebody to take back we don't know what shape they're in for swimming."

"How about we just ford the river—ride down the other side?"

"Stoney claims the banks are ten feet steep up here. He said we could do it about ten miles south, which is where Ortega probably crossed. Bill, we don't have time to ride any ten miles. Not if this General is the stickler for details I'm guessing him to be."

"I say the best bet is to go back and collar Smith," Crown said then.

"Yeh," Jess grunted. The best bet would have been to never laid eyes on Cyril Smith, he thought, wondering anew how any one man could be the root of so much grief.

"My pony smells water," Crown announced. "Should we be at the river this soon?"

"Just about." His own horse wanted to pick up the pace, too, and the riders gave the animals their head. Then, up ahead, the color of the landscape changed slightly and moments later the men could make out the broad, twisting form of the Rio Blanco.

"Man, that water's runnin' swift," Crown said. "Gonna split your raft into fifty pieces."

Bogan was thinking the same thought as he dismounted and untied the dragline. When he had devised the plan back at the ranch it had seemed impractical at best. Now, standing on the banks of the turbulent river, it looked impossible. Crown had his line undone, stood holding it in his hand, waiting.

"Let's ease her down the bank," Jess said without confidence. "Probably won't even float."

"That'd be your good luck, son. *Wooee*—looka that water go by!"

The bank was steep and the haphazard flatboat went down toward her launching almost eagerly. The front half went into the river, seemed to be heading directly for the bottom, then bobbed up again.

"Damn thing didn't sink," Crown said.

"Let's get her all in, but hang on to your line." They eased the rest of the raft into the river and instantly the tug on the lines became considerable. "Hold fast," Bogan said, leaning out from the bank to rest both hands tentatively on the primitive craft. It supported him. He swung one knee on board, still testing, then gave a push that landed him belly down on the raft. It swayed precariously, but as he inched forward the spread of his weight brought it to an even keel again.

123

"How you doin', boy?"

"So far so good. You can toss those lines on and let 'er rip." Crown threw the first line, and the sudden release made the raft swing wildly. Bogan grabbed hold of two planks with his hands and waited for the surge that would follow when the second rope set it free.

"Move over, damnit!" Crown yelled instead, throwing himself down beside Bogan in the same instant that he let go entirely of the line. That was four hundred pounds-plus, and the end of the raft shot almost straight up in the air. Bogan braced his foot against Crown's solid hip, pushed himself up the incline and got a purchase on the pine log. That end settled back down in the river and the raft immediately began cruising with the powerful current.

"Turn her around, Bill!" Bogan ordered. "Pull hard!" Holding to the log with one arm, he submerged the other up to the elbow in the water and began to paddle mightily. After two long, long minutes they finally overcame the force of the current and began making slow headway upstream. "There's a channel in the middle," he told Crown. "Work in close to that far bank."

Work it was, but when they were over to that side their progress became steadier. Bogan knew now that the raft would have been a staggering chore to manage alone in this powerful river and Crown's change of heart, if that's what it was, filled him with a solid, unspoken gratitude. Crown, for his part, kept up a steady flow of dire predictions and self-criticism.

"What a way to end up! Drownin'! Bogan, I can't swim a lick. Whatinhell am I doin' out here?"

"Keep it low," Jess told him. "We're near." This was a vague guess, but not five minutes later they rounded a bend and saw the lights of a fire some three hundred feet away. Silhouetted by the flame were a dozen or more figures, some moving back and forth on horseback, some on foot. The river widened measurably where the Mexicans were, and the banks loomed even higher and steeper, convincing Bogan that if there was one attempt at rescue possible in the time allotted this would be it. He was thinking that when he noticed that the activity in Ortega's camp had suddenly increased.

GUNS OF REVENGE

Mario Lazar reached down and shook the sleeping Ortega gently.

"What is it?"

"Their time is up, General. They are not coming with El Ingles."

"So be it," Ortega said heavily, climbing to his feet. His hawklike face was stern and unyielding, the expression of a man committed irrevocably to an action that he felt was right, but at the same time unpleasant. He stepped away from his blankets, walked in the direction of a huge cottonwood that overhung the river bank. There the campfire glowed, and nearby, loosely guarded, lay the frightened Carl Barthen. For some time now his captors had been describing in just-recognizable English, how it was to be hung to death, what an unforgettable experience he had in store unless his father gave up the Englishman. Their macabre humor included an introduction to a fat, grinning man named Pobrecito. Pobrecito, Carl was told, had been just a lowly cook for the General before the war. But then his real talents had been discovered, his artistry at fashioning the hangman's knot, at gauging a man's weight and the amount of drop necessary to break his neck satisfactorily.

Pobrecito, still grinning, had felt professionally of Carl's thighs and ribs, circled his neck with pudgy fingers and then let the grin dissolve into an expression of concern.

His hanging was not going to be very pleasant, Carl heard. Weights should be attached to his ankles, but alas, there were no such weights available here. Nor could Pobrecito guarantee a clean 'snap!' with such a slender neck to work with. All that the ex-cook could be sure of was that Carl would die at the end of the rope. Eventually.

"A brave man dies but once," Carl kept repeating to himself, but the picture had been painted in his mind too vividly by the Mexicans. He was dying once every ten minutes, each time more grotesquely than the last.

All at once the quiet, somnolent camp stirred to life and Carl found himself staring up into the face of El Lupo, for all the world like a figure fresh from the Inquisition. Roberto stood by as interpreter.

"You have borne arms against me as a bandit," Ortega

125

said to him. "The punishment for that offense is to hang. Do you have anything to say?"

"I thought my father was in the right," Carl answered in a drained voice.

"Your father is a shameless man," Ortega said, though the strength of the epithet was lost in translation. "But you are also going to die for another of your father's sins. He has chosen to defend the life of a traitor to my country . . ."

"I can't help that," Carl protested. Roberto translated and Ortega looked even grimmer.

"No, la culpa no es tuyo," Ortega said gravely. "It is not your fault. And may your father dwell on that when your body is brought to him." The General raised his hand. Two men standing behind Carl reached down and pulled him erect while a third lashed his wrists behind his back. Carl's wound, a rib graze, made him groan sharply at the rough treatment. He was then led, stumbling, to a place beneath the tallest branch of the tree. A small monkey of a man clambered up into the tree, carrying the ends of two long lengths of rope tied to his belt, and didn't stop climbing until he had reached the high branch. He unfastened both ropes, passed them over the branch and then, with the ease of much practice, casually lowered himself to the ground again with the help of two companions on the ground who payed out the rope against his negligible weight.

Pobrecito was holding the ends of both lines in his hands and now he waddled forward. One he slipped around Barthen's thin chest, beneath his armpits, and knotted securely. The other was already knotted in the hangman's trademark. This one he dropped over Carl's head, fitted into position and tightened. Pobrecito nodded to Ortega and stepped out of the way. Ortega spoke and his son translated for the doomed man.

"This is a sad business," Carl was told, "and will be done as quickly as possible. The chest rope will bear you to the topmost branch. Then it will be cut and you will drop until the slack is taken in the hang rope. *Vaya con Dios!*"

That was the signal for four of them to start Carl on

his last journey. When they had raised him some twelve feet from the ground Pobrecito motioned for the second rope to be started. Twelve feet, the hangman calculated, would do the job, and then raised his eyes—as fascinated as the rest by the spectacle of an execution.

Luis Ortega made one short outcry and that was all as a great arm locked tight around his throat and he was dragged swiftly backwards. The vaqueros who heard it happen whirled in startled surprise, then froze at the sight of the giant who held their General helpless, at the other fierce-looking gringo who stood by with a drawn gun in his hand.

"Cuidado!" Bogan said with meaning. "Take care! I give you this life for that one. Lower the rope again."

The men holding the rope made no move at all. Bogan increased the pressure through the crook of his arm and Ortega's body stiffened dangerously.

"Bajan!" the man Mario ordered crisply. "Let it down!" That snapped them out of it and Carl's body was quickly lowered to the ground.

"Vayan! Get away!" Bogan told them then and Crown stepped among them with just the right amount of bravado to get away with such a desperate play. Neither hurrying nor dawdling, he slipped both ropes from Barthen's neck and body—and stared in consternation as the young man's knees buckled and he started to fall. Crown scooped him to his shoulder, carried him back to Bogan like a sack of flour.

"Go on, Bill!" Jess said in an urgent whisper.

"This part I don't like . . ."

"Go on!"

Crown darted a glance over his shoulder at the Mexican band, everyone of them poised to attack, bright-eyed. His own face dubious, he went on into the deep shadows with his burden. Behind him he left a silence so taut it throbbed against the ear-drums. Bogan did not dare speak into it for fear of breaking the spell that held all of them so motionless. His eyes caught Mario's, bore into the other man's face in a battle of wills. For they both knew Bogan's tenuous position. If Mario ordered him attacked he had no chance in this world of saving his life. And, if

127

Mario ordered him attacked, would Bogan take Ortega's life? That was what the Mexican was trying to decide—what Bogan knew he was trying to decide. Jess, for his part, had no idea whether he was going to kill Ortega or not when they came at him. So it went between them as they tried to look into each other's mind—second pounding after second. An eternal minute passed. Mario decided to take him.

A gun went off in the distance. Again.

"Lo matan!" Mario shouted. "Kill him!"

But Bogan had been waiting for Crown's signal. He had that fractional advantage and had already released Ortega and was sprinting for the raft before any kind of pursuit was organized. He had, also, the knowledge of the little cove where the raft was moored—and the blessed darkness. There was a great racket at his back, but a tumultuous one, disorganized.

"Shove off!" he called to Crown, spotting him down below. Carl Barthen was lying prone across the raft Crown stood holding the lines, and at Jess' command he started it toward the mainstream and lay athwart the planks himself. Bogan slid down the high bank, waded knee-deep into the river and caught up with them. Balancing his weight very carefully he slowly pulled himself on board. The strong current picked them up, all in their favor now, and they pulled steadily away from Ortega's camp.

Carl Barthen slept through the trip like a babe.

3

From the time Ortega's son had ridden away from the ranch, relations between Ben Barthen and Cyril Smith had come under considerable strain. This particularly grieved the Englishman, for in the Yankee cattleman he believed that he had finally fulfilled his destiny, found the elusive pot of gold at rainbow's end.

But in Barthen's agonizing mood of self-appraisal and soul-searching it was as though the other man didn't exist. He had returned to the *hacienda* and sat with his melancholy thoughts, unmindful of the two gunfighters who studied the map on the wall, not hearing their low conversation, not even knowing when they had left. Barthen had escaped to another world from theirs, to a time when every decision he made was the right one, when there were no mind-torturing afterthoughts.

Smith had joined him in the study then, tried to engage him in an optimistic discussion of his latest plan to crush El Lupo. It was no use. Barthen only stared at him balefully, maintained a cold silence. Nothing could rouse him from the depression he felt. Smith left him, went to his own room to contemplate the bleak future he now faced. An hour passed, another. Suddenly the heavy silence that hung over the place was disrupted by a commotion in the courtyard. Above the clatter of horses rose the high-pitched voice of old Stoney.

"They did it!" the wrangler cried. "By grannies, they pulled it off!" Other voices joined in. "Give 'em a hand there, boys! Easy does it now!"

Miriam heard the sounds, slipped from her bed and looked down on the scene from the balcony, just in time to see her husband being carried into the house. Her glance darted all around, but nowhere could she find Beau Conerley. With a sigh she dismissed the redheaded lover from her life, turned up the lamp by the mirror and began making herself presentable for expected visitors.

Cyril Smith came out of a fitful sleep in time to observe the return of Carl Barthen, to hear with a sinking feeling the calm voice of Jess Bogan.

"He's a little feverish and wore out, Stoney. Just get him to bed and that'll do him."

The voices were slow to rouse Ben Barthen from his reverie. He climbed out of his chair with an effort, walked from the study just as the strange entourage was mounting the staircase to the floor above. Stoney spotted his boss, waved his hat joyously.

"Gunfighters is good for somethin' after all, Ben!" he hollered. "They brought your boy back home!"

Barthen took a hesitant step toward them, another, and then new life shot through him and he closed the distance rapidly. His hands came to rest on his son's shoulders and he grasped them emotionally.

129

"Another chance," he whispered. "The Lord gave me another chance. . . ."

Carl stirred beneath the grip, opened his eyes and smiled wanly. "Thanks, Dad," he said. "I knew you wouldn't let me down."

Ben Barthen was about to deny any credit but Stoney broke in sharply.

"Up to bed with him, boys," he ordered. "Plenty of time tomorrow for talkin'." The cowhands continued climbing the stairs, were met at the door of the bedroom by Miriam.

"Here's your fightin' man, missy," Stoney told her. "We'll leave him to your kind treatment."

"But what will I do?" Miriam asked uncomfortably.

"Do what any natural woman would do," the wrangler said with impatience.

Carl was lowered onto the bed and the cowboys departed hastily, embarrassed by the sight of the boss' daughter-in-law in her revealing nightclothes. Stoney closed the door, went to join Ben Barthen down below and rejoice.

In the other wing of the house Fran Riker was calling for Mary. She came into his room with a bright smile.

"What's going on, anyhow?" Riker demanded peevishly. "What's happening?"

"Wonderful news, Fran," the girl said. "Jess and that other fellow went and got Mr. Barthen's son. He's back home—can you imagine?"

"Took him," Riker asked slowly, "from Ortega?"

"Apparently. The whole place seems to be suddenly very happy."

Riker was gazing at her steadily, his expression deeply thoughtful.

"What is it, Fran? What's the matter?"

"Come sit by me, Mary," he said. "Come put your hand in mine while I tell you something."

"But it's so late, Fran. Can't it wait?"

"No," he said, "it can't. If I don't say this now I won't be able to sleep at all tonight."

"This old bunk don't look *very* good," Bill Crown said,

falling into the cot gratefully. He yawned mightily. "Bogan," he said, "next time you want to go for a boat ride in the middle of the night, count me the hell out. I'll ride withya, fight withya, dig gold till my back breaks. But, buddy, no more damn stunts on the water."

Jess didn't laugh at him or make any comment. That made Crown raise his head. "What's the matter now?" the easygoing gunman asked.

Jess was standing in the center of the lamplighted bunkhouse, counting heads. There were eight in here altogether.

"What's wrong, Bogan?" Crown asked again.

"There's no patrol out," Jess said. "No sentry."

"There's no ramrod around either," the man named Rogero reminded him. "Why the hell should we go out there on our own hook?"

"Only to save your life, friend," Bogan told him easily. "That's all." He slapped the gunfighter on the shoulder, pushed past him.

"Where you goin'?"

"To save my life——" The bunkhouse door swung in against him. Ben Barthen stood there.

"Hello, Bogan," he said.

"Hi."

"I came over to pay my respects." He held out his hand and Bogan took it briefly. "Where's Crown?"

"Crown's sleepin', boss," Crown said. Barthen walked toward the bunk.

"The boss is grateful," he said humbly. Then he swung around; a slim, small figure in the dimly lit room. "Spread Eagle pulls out in the morning," he told the guncrew. "Back to the home ranch." There was emotion in every word and now he cleared his throat, paused before speaking again. "I'm cutting myself down to size," Barthen said. "Every man present can have his two hundred acres in Arizona. First pick to Crown and Bogan."

There was a stirring among them, a murmuring, for what Barthen offered was the secret, never spoken dream of every drifting gunfighter—a quiet, peaceful little spread of his own; a few hundred head to run; a modest house with a woman inside it; not a gun in plain sight.

131

"Put me down for a little piece at Gila Bend," said the suddenly wide-awake Crown. "My friend Bogan will file next door."

Jess laughed. "Us new freeholders," he said to Barthen, "better start for Arizona sooner than morning."

"Why, Bogan?"

"Ortega," Jess answered flatly.

"You think he'll hit us here?"

"I'm guessing that he's through playing games with you," Bogan said. "And there ought to be somebody out there to give us some kind of warning." He started through the doorway a second time, quickly ducked back in. "Too late," he said even as a score of rifles smashed the night's quiet. Slugs thudded against the adobe walls, came screaming through the windows.

Crown swore a violent oath, dove from his bunk to the safety of the floor. The rest of the experienced crew made hard targets of themselves away from the openings.

"We've got to get out," Bogan said. "If we let him pin us down in here we're finished." He laid his carbine across the sill, triggered two shots. Another barrage hit the bunkhouse immediately. Bullets snarled their way into the wooden beams, smashed the oil lamp. "Go!" Bogan shouted. "Straight for the main house!" and began firing again through the window. The crew, led by Barthen, poured into the night, made a beeline for the *hacienda* some hundred and fifty feet away.

"Come on, Bogan, let's go!" Crown shouted and Jess looked over his shoulder to find the man helping with the covering fire from another window. At the same moment a bright flame leaped from a bunk where a blanket was ignited by the broken lamp. The straw mattress went up with a whoosh, spread the fire to the next bunk.

"Let's go!" Crown said again, pulling Bogan by the arm. At the doorway he paused for a second, crouched, then ran for it. Jess counted to three and followed. Crown suddenly pitched forward on both knees, tried to rise, stumbled another few steps and fell a second time. Jess knelt beside him, got the man's arm around his shoulder and rose with him as bullets kicked around them like so many angry hornets. Halfway from the *hacienda* Mc-

GUNS OF REVENGE

Crillus and Rowe met them, speeded the trip to the main house.

All of Spread Eagle was gathered in there, and Crown, amazingly, was the lone casualty of El Lupo's raid. Jess laid him out on a divan, cut away the trouser leg and examined the wound. The bullet had entered the calf, cracked the shin bone and passed on through. Jess bandaged it with a linen napkin, fashioned a splint from a box and told him to rest.

"Rest, hell! Just set me by a window and put a rifle in my hand. I got an idea we're in for it."

"We probably are," Bogan agreed. "Mr. Ortega's got himself this close to home and he ain't going to leave."

4

General Ortega intended to make things grimmer for Spread Eagle than even Jess Bogan realized. For while a portion of his band was trying to hold the gunfighters within the bunkhouse another group was scavenging for guns and ammunition. What they found, locked in the stifling storeroom, was the half-dead, half-demented Miguel. The man, mumbling incoherently, was brought before Ortega and the story of his torture and confinement was laboriously pieced out. One thing Miguel said was very clear: *"El Ingles."*

If Ben Barthen had caught an enemy and killed him, Ortega would have understood. But this that had been done to Miguel was a barbarous act—and with all his men looking on, the proud El Lupo vowed that Spread Eagle would atone for it in blood.

"Spare nothing," he told them, "spare no one. If we must destroy the *hacienda* to kill them, then we will destroy it. Follow me for Miguel!"

So saying, the General put spurs to his white stallion, sent it on a headlong flight directly against the great doors of the house. Behind him, wildly cheering, rode a dozen other horsemen. Behind them, on foot, a dozen more frenzied Mexicans. The white horse covered the steps in a leap, bounded across the porch and threw its weight sidewise against the wooden doors. The stout hinges

133

groaned under the assault but held firm. Another horse and rider slammed into it. A third. The doors sprung wide, presenting a sight to the men inside that was nearly overwhelming.

"Fight, Spread Eagle!" Ben Barthen cried. "Fight!"

But his gun crew had spread itself thin throughout the big house, expecting an infiltration rather than a direct attack, and Ortega's bold onslaught took them by surprise. Only ranch hands stood against him in the hallway, willing enough but woefully ineffective, and Ortega's furious horsemen swept among them, shooting with one hand, slashing their broad machetes murderously with the other. Ortega cut his way toward Barthen, rode him down without mercy, then looked everywhere for Smith.

He spotted the Englishman on the landing above, fired wildly at him as Smith fled for cover. One of his own men was abruptly driven from his saddle, then another, as Bogan and company joined the fray with their accurate, unhurried shooting. Ortega saw the quick advantage of his surprise foray diminishing.

"*Salimos, salimos!*" he ordered. "Out, out!" and led the way from the house, losing two more riders but leaving behind ten dead or wounded of his enemies. Ortega regrouped his force near the brightly blazing bunkhouse and set them to lighting *palos del fuego,* burning pieces of wood which one horseman after another took to the *hacienda* and flung toward an open window.

A flaming stick landed in the bedroom of Carl and Miriam. The drapes took fire instantly, raced upward to the wooden beams across the ceiling. The girl ran screaming into the corridor just as Bogan was rushing toward the room.

"It's on fire!" she shouted hysterically. "We'll be killed!"

Jess pulled her hands from his shirt, pushed past her into the room and yanked the drapes down from their rings, stomped on them until the flame was out. From the bureau he took a pitcher of water, flung its contents against the ceiling to extinguish the blaze there. He started back out of the room but Miriam barred his way.

"What's going to happen to us?" she demanded.

"I wish I knew," Jess said, his voice tight.

"But I didn't do anything!" she screamed at him hysterically. "I'm not a part of this!"

"You are now, sister," he told her.

"But I didn't do anything! I don't want to die!"

"You got a lot of company," Jess said, moving her aside. Then, over the head of the terrified Miriam, he found himself looking into the calm, beautiful face of Mary Washen. It was as if in the midst of all this strife she had found something to make her happy. The girl's eyes fairly glowed into his.

Jess stepped to her.

"Fran told me what happened this afternoon," she said. "And he said—he said to tell you that he's not the right man after all."

Jess laid his hands on her shoulders, felt the strength of her flow into his fingers. They smiled at each other and that seemed to be all the communication they needed.

"*Bogan!* Hey, Bogan!" somebody yelled from downstairs, needing help.

"I have to get down there," Jess said.

"I know. What can I do to help?"

Bogan slid his Colt from the holster, handed it to her. "They may try to scale the balcony around back," he said. "You see anything in a sombrero, shoot it."

"Yes, sir," Mary said and Bogan grinned, squeezed her shoulder another time. Then she quickly turned and went to the far wing while he descended the stairs. Fire was the major trouble down here, too. Small blazes everywhere, and no sooner was one put out but another started. Ortega harassed them that way for a long exhausting hour, then ordered a pause.

The sudden quiet out there was nerve-wracking to some.

"Why don't he hit again and get it over with?" Rogero asked nobody in particular.

"Hell, yes," Heilman agreed. "Let's shoot it out."

"How about we parley with the sonofabitch?" Rowe suggested. "The old man's dead—what argument we got with the Mex?"

"You savvy the lingo good, Bogan,' Wightman said. "What do you say we call it a draw and go home?"

135

"Whatever you boys want," Jess told them. "Crown?"

The wounded man grinned, slipped a shell nonchalantly into the chamber of his rifle.

"War or peace," he said obligingly. "Anything suits me but this goddamn waiting."

"All right," Bogan said. "I'll see if I can find out what this General figures he's going to win." A truce flag was fashioned from a sheet and Jess ventured out of the *hacienda* with it. Now the silence had an eerie, threatening atmosphere about it, and as Bogan's heels sounded on the flagstones of the courtyard he could feel his stride being carefully measured by a dozen riflemen in the darkness.

"Alto!" commanded a stern voice suddenly and Jess halted in his tracks. "Do you surrender, hombre?"

"Hell, no," Jess answered quietly. Ortega, mounted, came out of the shadows followed by three others.

"Then why do you come out here with that white flag?"

"To talk a little sense to you, mister," Jess said. "None of us in there are going to throw down. We're not worried."

"Every man wants to live," Ortega said.

"Not that way," Bogan answered. "Not that bunch of boys. And all you're going to get out of it is to see your fine house burn to the ground. That's the straight of it, Ortega."

The don raised his eyes from Bogan's face and gazed at his *hacienda*. The *Casa Ortega* was one hundred and fifty years old, four generations of his family had been born under its roof.

"Very well," the General said then. "You are permitted to leave. All but the Englishman."

"And the blonde woman," said another voice, ominously.

"The woman is with her husband," Bogan said.

"No me importa," Mario said. "I want the woman."

Bogan shook his head. "She goes when we do," he said. A moment later he was looking into the muzzle of Mario's gun.

"And where do you think *you're* going, hombre?" Mario

asked him. Jess shifted his glance to Ortega's stern face. *"Que pasa?"* he said. "What's going on?"

"This morning you took one of my men prisoner," Ortega said coldly. "Miguel by name."

"That's right."

"Mario is brother to Miguel."

There was something in the way that was said that made the hairs along Bogan's neck ripple.

"What happened to Miguel?" he asked softly.

"Hombre, to have killed him would have been an act of mercy."

Bogan shook his head from side to side, feeling a sick anger at Cyril Smith.

"I didn't know," he said. "So many things have been going on . . ."

"I will have El Ingles," Ortega said. "Mario desires the woman. The rest of you can go—"

Miriam Barthen's scream pierced the night. Guns exploded inside the house. Bogan whirled to see sombreroed figures swarming into the rear of the place, to see two of them framed in the upper floor window, grappling with Carl Barthen.

"Bogan, come back! Bogan!" It was Crown calling to him, and with a vision of Mary's face flashing through his mind, Jess broke into a dead run. Mario fired. The bullet seared Bogan's rib, staggered him for an instant.

"Enough!" Ortega shouted behind him. "He carried the flag!" But the truce didn't extend to those inside and Ortega led the charge toward the house. Horses pounded past Bogan, their riders yelling wildly, as if they sensed victory. Jess plunged on in their wake, his whole left side a white hot fire. The fighting up ahead was building to a furious crescendo and all he could see were Ortega's men. They seemed to be everywhere.

He reached the steps of the veranda as a hideously yelling body came hurtling from a window above and struck the courtyard not three feet behind him. Jess turned to see that it was Cyril Smith, with the hilt of an eight-inch dagger protruding from his back. He looked up then to Miguel, who leaned far out over the balcony rail and

137

grinned down in triumph at his victim.

And overriding every other sound, punctuating it, was the screaming, terrified voice of Miriam Barthen. Jess slid the .45 he had borrowed from its holster, went on into the melee inside. Very vaguely he was aware of another commotion at his back, of a sound very much like thunder, and someone shouting *"Soldados! Soldados!"*

He got through the doorway and the first thing he saw was Bill Crown, his shirtfront soaked with blood, penned into a corner by three Mexicans. Bogan opened up on one, dropped him, triggered two more slugs into a second. Then he caught a second wound of his own, in the thigh, and the impact dropped him to one knee. A little blurrily he saw Crown take out his third assailant on his own.

Jess forced himself to stand again, limped his way to the staircase and started to climb upstairs.

"Soldados! Soldados!" someone kept yelling, frenziedly outside and men in sombreros were running this way and that way. Bogan glanced up the stairs to see Mario on the landing above, struggling with the half-naked Miriam. Jess fired once and the Mexican stiffened and came hurtling toward him. Jess got out of his way and continued on up there. The blonde was slumped on the floor, sobbing wildly, but Bogan had no time to comfort her.

There was gunfire down in the far wing, a lot of it, and Jess reloaded as he made his slow, painful way in that direction.

"Hang on, Mary!" he heard his voice shouting crazily. "Hang on!" Three of Ortega's men were involved and they were laying siege to an open doorway. At the sound of Bogan's voice one of them whirled and fired at him. He answered it from a crouched position, turned the .45 on the other pair. Suddenly there was nothing else to shoot at and the corridor fell silent. Jess stood up again, dizzily.

"Mary!" he called, moving forward like a drunken man. "Mary . . ." There was a blurred figure standing in the doorway. Then it was hurrying toward him.

"Oh, Jess!" the girl cried joyously.

"You're all right?"

"Yes," she said, "I'm all right. And so is Fran. But

we had fired our last bullet. They would have come in for
us in the next moment."

Jess grinned foolishly and started to go down. The last
thing he remembered hearing was *"Soldados! Soldados!"*
Whatever the hell that meant.

2

The orders for First Lieutenant Harmon, commanding
A Company, Fifth Regiment, were to pull his troopers
back to El Centro and take with him all United States citi-
zens who requested evacuation. The new border was settled
and the peace between the countries was finally signed,
which suited the Lieutenant fine. For some time now he
had been wondering if the Army was going to leave A
Company in this godforsaken no man's land forever, if
he was ever going to get back to civilization. He ordered
the camp struck and within an hour the happy cavalry
detachment was enroute north. The Lieutenant, mindful
of his orders, meant to pay a call on the rancher, Barthen,
though he knew beforehand that is was going to be a waste
of time. The cattleman and his crew would refuse point-
blank to leave the country, though it was obvious now
that Barthen's position was legally and politically impossible. The man would hang on stubbornly, the soldier
figured, but pretty soon he would have to defend himself
against the Mexican army itself. . . .

Then, directly ahead, came the sound of wild firing and
excited shouts.

"Sounds like a big fight," Harmon's orderly said.

"Better have a look-see," Harmon said, spurring his
mount to a fast trot. A Company responded immediately,
and within minutes it fell upon the rear of Ortega's fighters.
The Mexicans, badly startled, swung around and opened
fire. A cavalryman was knocked from his saddle, another
groaned, and even if the Lieutenant wanted to he could
not have kept his angry men from charging headlong into
the fray. A withering burst dropped half a dozen Mexicans
in their tracks. More fell before the next volley, and those
that didn't go down ran full tilt toward the beseiged house,

shouting the warning to those fighting Barthen's crew inside.

But Don Luis Ortega, from the balcony of the master bedroom, had already seen the wave of blue riders sweeping toward him. Saw the disciplined American troop and knew that his already badly mauled band was in a hopeless situation. All that resistance meant now was sure death in a cause that, right or wrong, was lost. The slender man moved to the balcony rail, raised both arms above his head in the traditional gesture of surrender, and ordered his men to throw down their arms.

At that, Lieutenant Harmon had the bugler sound the cease fire and the fighting stopped as abruptly as it had started. Ortega descended to the main floor, but when he went to unbuckle the saber at his side and present it to the young officer he was surprised to see Harmon shake his head vigorously.

"I don't want your sword, *Señor*," Harmon said. "So far as I'm concerned I'm standing in your house on Mexican soil."

"Do my ears deceive me?' Don Luis asked incredulously. "Your government is giving me back what is mine?"

Harmon nodded. "All I want, *Señor,* is safe conduct out of your country with these nationals. We leave in peace."

It was the jouncing, more than anything else, that made Jess Bogan open his eyes again. He found himself being carried in a large wagon, one with a green tarpaulin top, and the bright morning sunlight made the letters 'U.S.A.' stand out very clearly.

But if that was clear, nothing else was. He turned his head to see that Bill Crown was stretched out beside him, eyes closed tight and body motionless. Bogan started to reach with his left hand, found that painful and used his right instead to explore Crown's chest for a heartbeat.

"Hell, I ain't dead," Crown announced peacefully.

"Glad to hear that. What are we doing?"

"Getting a ride back to the States."

"That's nice. And who arranged it?"

Crown told him about the arrival of the troopers and the armistice with Ortega.

"And damn lucky, too," he said. "Man, I had Mexes just about comin' out my ears."

"I remember," Jess said. "Anybody else making the trip?"

"Riker's back there in a wagon. And McCrillus. Just the four of us from the gun crew."

"Barthen's son?"

"Dead. The widow's been lookin' in on you pretty regular."

Jess glanced sideways at the other wounded man. "Any other visitors?"

"Some big soldier about the size of you. Sergeant name of Bronco. He sticks his ugly mug in here about every fifteen minutes."

"Anybody else?"

"Just your girl—Mary Washen," Crown said.

"My *girl?*"

"That's what she calls herself," Crown told him. "Did you know you're gonna ranch over in Arizona?"

"No," Jess said, "I didn't."

Crown grinned at him. "She'll tell you all about it when she comes back with chow," he said. "The free and easy life is over for you, Bogan."

Jess closed his eyes and smiled. It sounded fine to him.

THE END

141

*He Was Called "Devil" Devlin—The Man
Who Could Tame The Wildest Town!*

TOWN MARSHAL

By Don Catlin

Author of THE TROUBLE SHOOTER

Town Marshal "Devil" Devlin felt like a man sitting
on an open powder keg while smoking a cigar. Sun-
stroke, Arizona Territory, was infested with outlaws,
rustlers and murderers.

Ore wagons and stages were constantly looted, the
guards drygulched. And marshals had a way of dying
at the hands of "persons unknown." It was an organized attack on law and order—and somewhere
one man plotted it all, manipulating the puppets who
did his bidding.

Cleaning up the town would be a Herculean task, but
Devlin decided to do it. He would show no mercy, for
the bad ones respected only one thing on earth—
intolerant, arrogant, domineering force.

And if the "man at the top" proved to be the man
Devlin had been seeking for five long years, so much
the better. At last he might be able to lay to rest his
need for violent vengeance.

A New Topnotch Western Novel from

MONARCH BOOKS, INC.

Available at all newsstands and bookstores   35¢

If you are unable to secure this book at your local dealer, you
may obtain a copy by sending 35¢ plus 5¢ for handling to
Monarch Books, Inc., Mail Order Department, Capital Building,
Derby, Connecticut.

There Was An Ambush Around Every
Bend And Death Behind Every Rock

THE LAST OUTLAW

By Bennett Garland

Author of HIGH STORM

A   M O N A R C H   W E S T E R N   N O V E L

WANTED! For Bank Robbery And Interference With The United States Mails: THE CARDEEN BROTHERS.

No one knew that they were outlaws by accident rather than choice. They separated, only to have fate bring them together again in a brutal range war: Joe as a hired gunslinger with the sheepmen, Logan on the side of the cowmen, and Emmett caught in the middle. For Emmett it was a difficult decision to make.

Which brother should he side? Which one could he more easily face and kill if it came to a showdown?

> **MONARCH Westerns Are The Best Your Money Can Buy. Read These Novels And See For Yourself!**

Available At All Newsstands and Bookstores

If you are unable to secure these or other MONARCH BOOK titles at your local dealer, you may obtain copies by sending price of books, plus 5¢ per copy for handling to:

MONARCH BOOKS, Inc.

Capital Building   Derby, Connecticut 06418

Mail Order Department 164

The Dramatic Saga Of The
Greatest Of All The Indian Tribes

THE CHEYENNE WARS

By Joseph Millard

A M O N A R C H A M E R I C A N A B O O K

For decades the Cheyenne Indians endured abuses from the white settlers without spilling a single drop of white blood in well-merited reprisal. Finally, goaded beyond human endurance, they turned on their tormentors with all the pent-up ferocity of their savage natures. Hungry, homeless and driven, the Cheyennes repeatedly defeated overwhelming forces of well-equipped troops, to win the accolade: "The finest natural cavalry on earth."

Don't fail to read this saga of a mighty people, as well as these other popular MONARCH AMERICANA books about the Indian wars: